MW01097671

SHOW STOPPER

BJ HARVEY

Show Stopper

Copyright © 2020 by BJ Harvey

Edited by Lauren Clarke

Cover Designed by BJ Harvey

Photo sourced from Shutterstock

ISBN: Kindle— 978-0-6487638-4-0

ISBN: Epub— 978-0-6487638-3-3

ISBN: Print— 978-0-6487638-8-8

Without limiting the rights under copyright reserved above, no part of this publication may be reproduced, stored in or introduced into a retrieval system, or transmitted, in any form, or by any means (electronic, mechanical, photocopying, recording, or otherwise) without the prior written permission of the above author of this book.

This is a work of fiction. Names, characters, places, brands, media, and incidents are either the product of the author's imagination or are used fictitiously. The author acknowledges the trademarked status and trademark owners of various products referenced in this work of fiction, which have been used without permission. The publication/use of these trademarks is not authorized, associated with, or sponsored by the trademark owners.

✳ Created with Vellum

1

RENEE

One thing that doesn't work in your favor when you're a real estate agent is a propensity for always running late.

Unfortunately for me, it's a Friday when I have back-to-back property showings and my alarms—all three of them—were all miraculously snoozed, and I now have only forty minutes to shower, dress, do my makeup, pour coffee down my throat and get out my front door. Because no house sales means no commission, which means no roof over my head, sexy heels on my feet or Starbucks in my hand, and I need all those things.

Walking into the kitchen, having done the shower, makeup, and half of the dressing side of my to-do list, I spot my bleary-eyed sister Hayley staring off out the window, cradling a mug of steaming caffeine nectar in her hands. Hayley moved to Chicago from Wisconsin four months ago after a nasty breakup with her ex-boss, which led to her being let go from her job at the same time.

"You're late," she says without looking at me.

"No shit, Sherlock." I walk over to the coffee machine, quickly making myself a caramel macchiato with far more caramel than my hips need. But the maintenance of my curves is a serious business, and if caramel is the key, then I'm a devoted follower to testing and proving this theory to be true.

"Guess I better add caramel syrup to the grocery list," my sister mumbles from behind me.

I snicker and face her, mimicking her pose with my coffee cup as I lean back against the kitchen counter. "You? Do the shopping?"

"I am capable of running errands, you know." I arch a brow, making her gasp. "I take offence to that. I can adult. . . occasionally."

"And apparently pigs can fly and the moon landing was a big, giant hoax."

Her lips twitch as she takes a slug of coffee from her mug.

"Not going in today?" I ask, before taking my much-needed over-sugared caffeine hit.

Hayley is a free-spirited wild child and has been since the day she was born. She lives life on her terms, on her schedule, and can some-times have issues with authority. That has included calling off work because she doesn't feel like it.

"Late start." Hayley works in the front office for the Chicago Fire soccer team. "It's the team's travel day so my boss said to take the morning off. There's not much to do anyway."

"Nice." I take a quick look at my watch and a big gulp of my drink. "Shit. I really have to go. I've got a showing just after lunch, and I need to go into the office first to get the marketing materials John made up for me. I also wanted to call in and see Grams quickly."

"And how is John?"

I grimace. "Still asking me out once a week, but it's more a case of, 'when are you going to put me out of my misery',' nothing else."

My sister screws her face up. "Yeah. There's sugar daddy, and then there's John. Far too old."

I nod. "And I'm not into stirring the company pot."

"That too," she says, her lips curving up. "I definitely learned *that* lesson. Hey, maybe you'll have some hot bachelor come to your showing and sweep you off your feet."

"One can only hope," I say with a snort. "But it's very unlikely. Besides, dating a potential buyer probably isn't overly professional."

Hayley rolls her eyes. "Look at you being all responsible."

"Someone's got to be," I say, poking my tongue out. "I've really got to go. I'll see you later?"

"Well, duh. It's Real Housewives of Everywhere night. I'll grab the takeout on the way home, since the maid hasn't done the grocery shopping," she adds with a wink.

"Maybe the maid is waiting to see if her counterpart will do it for her."

"That can be arranged . . . for a fee . . ."

I quirk a brow. "And that would be?"

"A blind date. We've got a new player who's just been traded to the team, and he's single and ready to mingle in the big city."

"Hayley," I groan. "You know I'm not interested in being set up with anyone." She gives me a guilty grin and I narrow my eyes. "Why do I feel like you've already arranged this?"

"Not exactly . . ." she says, averting her gaze. "He's cute, if that helps, and his arms? Damn. Those babies could do a lot of heavy lifting."

"And on that note, I'm out of here." I cross the kitchen and kiss her cheek before grabbing my purse off the hallway table and moving to the front door.

"You didn't say no," she calls as I'm halfway out.

"I didn't say yes, either," I retort, giving her a quick wave before leaving. Having a sister with the best of intentions may actually be the death of me.

———

Three hours later, I'm waiting in the kitchen for the clock to tick past one p.m. so I can open the front door and hopefully welcome in a hoard of potential buyers for this listing—a three-bedroom duplex near Palmer Square.

It has enormous potential, but when I took the deceased estate listing, I knew it could go either way in terms of being an easy sell or one of those tricky properties that sit on the market for a while. I'm always up for a challenge, though, so I jumped at the chance.

It's been a slow start, but with effective but inexpensive staging that the daughter of the former owner was more than happy to front up for, a few well-placed vases of fresh fragrant flowers, and the gentle scent of a French vanilla candle wafting through the air, I'm confident that today's showing—albeit, the third for this house—will be a well-received one.

A car door closing on the street outside grabs my attention, and after a quick look in my compact mirror, I take a deep breath, stow away my purse in a kitchen cabinet, and walk through to the front entryway, swinging the door open, signaling that the house is open for viewing.

The first couple of parties are the real estate equivalent of tire kickers—people who aren't in the market to buy, but like to have a good look. I can usually pick them a mile away, but a telltale sign is when they're hesitant to leave their details on the call sheet. I still treat them as potential buyers though because you never know when they might decide they're ready to commit to a new property, and you might cross paths with them at another time in another house. If that happens, you already have that name-recognition/first-impression in the bag. That's my theory, anyway.

With ten minutes to go and no more parties coming through, I begin to think the showing is a bust when the roar of a car outside grabs my attention. Deciding I'm not ready to write this day off just yet, I go to the front porch, ready to greet what could be another potential buyer.

Which is fine if you're not wearing four-inch Jimmy Choo heels and a knee-length pencil skirt, and you trip on the first step with a huge smile plastered on your face. I scream as I go flying off the front stairs, my arms flailing and my eyes clenched shut as I brace myself for impact, expecting the worst.

Except I don't hit the ground. Instead, there's a loud muttered "damn" just before I hit a wall of someone, the two of us crashing backwards as we both fall down in a tangle of limbs onto the front lawn. The stranger lands first, a loud groan escaping him followed by a low grunt when I land on top of him at my most unladylike best.

We lie there unmoving for a few moments until my eyes snap open. Mortification hits. I lift my head and look down at him, my lips parting to say thank you when I'm rendered speechless by the concerned—and absolutely mesmerizing—deep chocolate gaze shining back at me.

"Are you okay?" he asks roughly, and I swear, I have a mini-orgasm from the sound of his voice alone. I stare down at him, rendered mute for what seems like hours before the man looks around us then returns his amused gaze to mine.

"Well, that didn't go quite how I planned," he says with a cheeky grin. "Now I'm all for public displays of affection, but I'm not sure if this was the kind of showing you had in mind. Not that I'm complaining at having a beautiful woman lying on top of me."

That snaps me out of it.

"Shit," I say, rolling off and away from him and scrambling to my knees. He jumps to his feet as quick as a flash and leans down, placing his hands on my hips. He lifts me back to my feet as if I weigh nothing.

As soon as I'm back upright, blood flow must return to my brain because I finally regain my ability to think straight. "I'm so sorry. It's lucky you were here to cushion my fall though," I say with a laugh.

He smiles and dips his chin, looking down between us and slowly pulling his arms away from where he was holding me steady. I didn't realize he was still touching me, and now all I can feel is the searing palm-print of where his hands have been. God, maybe I should go on that blind date.

Mystery man's lips curve into a sexy half grin. "You're welcome. It's not every day I get the chance to help a damsel in distress."

I snicker and cock my head to the side. "It's not every day a knight in shining armor saves me from making an absolute dick of myself in front of a potential buyer."

His smile widens. "I wouldn't say an absolute dick. Maybe I have a thing for women falling at my feet."

I arch a brow at him. "Hey, if it helps sell the house, I'll walk back up there and fall down all over again."

He chuckles, and I feel myself falling into a daze. Dammit, Ren. Stop swooning over the hot man.

"You don't need to go that far, although I'm not complaining. Any man would do the same if you were the one doing the falling."

I barely stop myself from fanning my face before I remember what I'm doing and what the man is here for. Sell the house, Ren. Don't flirt with the buyer.

I quickly switch back into professional realtor mode and flash him a dazzling you-know-you-want-to-buy-this-home smile.

"So, after that eventful introduction, I'm guessing you're here to see the house?"

"Should I walk behind you just in case I have to catch you again?," he says, making my knees wobble a little.

I laugh and shake my head. "I've been walking in heels since I was a kid stealing my mom's shoes to walk down the hallway. I think I'm good."

He stares at me, his eyes still warm, but there's something else in his gaze I can't pinpoint. I kind of hope it was lust, attraction, a desire to throw me against the nearest surface and ravish me until I'm a panting, breathless mess.

He lazily runs his eyes down to my silver pumps and back again, forcing me to fight off a full-on body shiver. "Still, I definitely won't complain if I have to follow you around. You know . . . just to be safe."

There's absolutely no mistaking the intent of his words now, and it's taking everything in me not to melt into a puddle at his feet. Since that would ruin my very expensive shoes, I lock my knees and decide I really need to move this along to avoid the risk of doing myself an injury by clenching my thighs too tightly.

"Right. So are you waiting for anyone else, or . . .?"

He opens his mouth to reply, but we're interrupted by a stunning blonde running up to us in an EMT uniform.

"Sorry, I'm late. I got caught in traffic. But I'm here now," she says, leaning in and giving the man an enormous bear hug, which he reciprocates. He smiles down at her lovingly and pulls her into his side. Damn, okay. That answers that question. Definitely taken. That is exactly the cold bucket of water I needed to cool my jets. Kind of douchey to flirt with me while waiting for his significant other.

"Right. Okay. Hi, I'm Renee. I'm the realtor for this house, and we were just about to go inside if you'd like to join us."

"Awesome. I'm Skye," she says, shaking my hand. She turns to the man I was just lying on top of. "I wanted to have a look at this one first before talking to you know who." The still nameless man chuckles, and I plaster an overstated smile to hide my reaction to his simple action.

What is it about a deep, low laugh that turns strong, kick-ass women to mush?

"Let's go inside, and you two can have a look around," I say, carefully walking up the stairs, feeling Mr. Possibly Married, Still Doesn't Have A Name, Was Flirting With Me And Clearly Has A Girlfriend, following behind me.

"Watch your step," he says, sounding amused.

"What did I miss?" Skye asks curiously from the back of the line.

"Oh, nothing, brat. Renee here is a bit shaky on her feet despite years of walking in heels, apparently."

"Damn, girl. Be careful. You don't want to break an ankle. But I will say, those Jimmy Choos are hot," Skye says, and I can't help but smile. It's hard to be envious of a woman with a sexy, smart-mouthed boyfriend when she's nice.

I look over my shoulder with a genuine smile on my face. "Thank you. They were my reward for reaching my sales targets last year. I only pull them out for special occasions. Like selling a house?" I say jokingly, waggling my brows.

"She's good, Marco. You better watch yourself. She'll try to get us to buy another house too," Skye says, walking past me and into the house.

Confused by her statement, I stumble—again—and Marco's hands come to my hips . . . again. Why is he touching me? Does he have no shame? Maybe they have an open relationship? I've been in an open relationship before and it wasn't fun. Granted, it was one-sided, mainly because I had no idea my fiancée was banging multiple women behind my back for years. Good riddance.

"I'm thinking you might need more practice in those shoes," he murmurs in my ear as I right myself.

"Or you could stop using my clumsiness as an excuse to touch me," I murmur quietly.

"Now, why would I want to do that? I'm just doing my job. I live to serve."

"Serving doesn't mean copping a feel every chance you get," I mutter, horrified at the fact I actually like the fact he's teasing me. Ugh. This is why I swore off men after my last disaster of a relationship.

I close my eyes, take a deep breath, put on my most professional, cheerful smile and turn around, stepping away from the man who has me not thinking straight.

"So, I'll let you guys have a look around at your own leisure, and I'll just be in the kitchen if you have any questions. Sound okay?"

Marco's eyes lock with mine. It's as if he's studying me—or reading my mind—which would be a terrible thing right now. Especially with his maybe sister, maybe girlfriend or wife standing right next to him. "C'mon, macho man," Skye says, grabbing his arm and pulling him into the front living room. "I need you to be the voice of reason. I don't want to take this back to the guys and have them think I'm bringing them a lemon."

"Just come find me if you need me," I call out, carefully walking backwards down the hallway towards the other end of the house.

"I will," Marco says, his eyes not leaving mine until he disappears from sight.

I'm left feeling off-kilter at the strange effect he's having on me. I don't flirt with potential clients, and I definitely don't flirt with possibly attached ones.

So maybe I'll just write this whole experience off as a friendly exchange and be done with it.

"Thank you, Renee," Skye says shaking my hand on their way out. "It's not quite what I was looking for—a bit too finished for our purposes—but I'll definitely keep your card in case we find ourselves in need of a realtor."

I grin. "Definitely do that. It was nice to meet you, though."

Marco doesn't say anything else to me, he simply smiles and follows Skye out the door.

Which probably explains why I'm still feeling out of sorts and yet weirdly amused while reviewing the call sheets from the day's showings later that night. I'm fixated on the last two names written down.

Skye Cook and Marco Rossi—two different addresses, two different phone numbers.

I might not even see them again. Regardless, I'll get my assistant to do a courtesy follow-up call to Skye, and since she's already said the property didn't fit the bill, that will probably be as far as it goes.

But what takes the cake is he had the balls to write "call me next time you want to be caught" next to his phone number. Right next to Skye's name. That screams player, and if my past has taught me anything, it's that I'm not interested in philanderers or players, no matter how sexy, charming, and funny the man may be.

No way. Not at all.

2

MARCO

"You've got to come out with us tomorrow night, Marco Polo," my colleague—and the biggest pain in my ass—Scotty says.

I turn my head and arch a brow. "Why?" I ask, my mouth full of an Italian beef sandwich. We got back to the firehouse twenty minutes ago and after a hectic afternoon, I'm taking the chance to eat while I can.

My brother Luca plops down on the bench seat beside me and snorts. "Because you pull in the chicks that wouldn't give him a chance otherwise."

Scotty flips Luca the bird. "Sit on that and rotate, Rossi."

I snicker and shake my head. "You know that could be offensive to me since I'm a Rossi too, right?"

Scotty rolls his eyes. "I wouldn't do that to my lieutenant. That would be disrespectful."

"But you'd do it to me?" Luca asks, brow quirked.

Scotty shrugs. "If the shoe fits."

My sister Skye and her husband, Cohen, walk into the big open-plan living area of the firehouse. They're partners in our station's ambulance, which makes Firehouse 101 a bit Rossi heavy considering that's three out of us five siblings working together. Lucky we all get along.

Skye comes up and wraps her arms around my shoulders, hugging me from behind. "Aww, come on, big brother. You're not too old to hit the clubs. . . not *yet* anyway."

The rest of the guys snicker and my lips twitch. "Thanks for that, brat."

She straightens, and I catch a mischievous twinkle in her eyes. "I saw for myself the other day how much you've still got it."

"Now *this* I want to hear," Scotty says, leaning forward in his seat.

"Marco came with me to view a house for sale and he already had the realtor on the ground and on top of him by the time I turned up."

I groan. "It wasn't like that."

"It was *totally* like that," she says. "Then he kept catching her when she stumbled."

"He probably just wanted to cop a feel," Scotty jokes.

Skye scrunches up her face. "Not all men are that desperate," she replies, poking her tongue out at him.

Scotty eyes me curiously. "What was she like?"

"She was . . ." No. I don't want to go back to thinking about that brunette firecracker. She occupied my brain for far too long this week, considering it was only a twenty-minute exchange and despite having my number, and the cheeky little invitation I'd written beside it, she has not called. I thought for sure she'd at least do a personal follow-up. Instead, her assistant called on her behalf. A little disappointing, but I'm a firm believer in things happening and people crossing paths for a reason. If something is meant to happen, I'll see her again sometime. *Hopefully*.

The bells ring out, saving me from answering but also signaling a frustratingly early end to our 'grab whatever you can and shove it in your mouth' meal break.

I take one final big bite of my roll before wrapping it and pushing up out of my seat, shooting Scotty a narrow glare. "Just remember, Scotty Jones, I can make life very difficult for you—in the firehouse and out of it."

"You wouldn't . . ." he says cockily, but there's an edge of concern to his voice now. "I was just messing around, Lieutenant. I didn't—"

I shrug and can't help but smirk. "Yeah. But you forget one thing, Scotty . . ." He's behind me now, following as we rush to the garage and step into our turnout gear. "I own your ass for twenty-four hours every three days. It pays not to piss me off. Especially if you want to use me to try and get yourself laid."

The rest of the crew chuckle.

"Yeah, yeah. Okay," he mutters, jerking his turnout pants up and hooking the suspenders over his shoulders. "So, you'll come then?"

"Who else is going? And where?" I ask.

"The whole crew and Throb."

I groan, shaking my head as I jump into the passenger seat of the truck. "That place is a meat market."

"Your point?" Luca asks, hopping in and shutting the driver's door when he's positioned behind the wheel.

My best friend, Rhodes, looks at me, his eyes dancing with amusement. "I'll go if you go."

I let out a resigned sigh. "Some of us are too old to go clubbing."

"Going out might improve your disposition a bit," Luca mutters loudly enough for the rest of the crew in the back to hear.

I fight back a laugh. "Heard that, asshole."

"Didn't whisper it, jerk-off," Luca retorts with a grin, turning the key and bringing the truck to life.

The garage doors jerk to a stop as they reach the top, and I grab hold of the oh-shit bar as my brother puts his foot down and we roll out, following the rescue truck in front of us.

Rhodes leans forward and puts a hand on my shoulder. "C'mon, Marky Mark, we haven't been out in a while, and I need someone to sit with me and watch these fools crash and burn as they try to score."

"Even Gio's coming. He never comes out anymore," Luca says, changing tack. Gio is our youngest brother, bookmarked between our middle sister, Valentina, and Skye.

I shake my head. "That's 'cause he's smart."

"It's also because he's a workaholic who doesn't care if he never gets laid again," Luca says with a chuckle. "Like someone else I know."

I smirk and turn my head Luca's way. "Oh, he gets laid." I always love when I know something he doesn't.

Luca's head jerks my way. "What?"

"Nothing," I say, quickly changing the subject because the guys in back don't need to know about Gio's private life. "So, back to tomorrow night. Is there a special occasion? Or are we just going out because we have two days off and Scotty is a horn dog?"

"It's ladies' night," Scotty yells from behind me.

"Ah. Now I get it. More ladies than men, Scotty included."

"Trying hard not to curse you again, boss," the man in question grumbles. He knows it's in good fun though. We've been working together for nine years now. After that long, we all give each other shit. It helps break up the long twenty-four-hour shifts together.

"Right. Good luck with that. I now might make it my mission to piss you off so you do something dumb, then I can take pleasure in the threat of writing you up."

"You wouldn't . . ." he gasps. I shrug.

"Who knows?" I try to keep a straight face but lose the fight, and a snicker escapes my lips.

"Such a dick," Scotty mutters.

"Heard that," I say. I look over my shoulder and smirk back at him. "Meant you to."

Rhodes points his arm straight ahead toward the windshield. "Ah, good chat, guys, but see that big plume of smoke right ahead? We kind of need to get there. They've called in five engines for this one."

I look out in front of us, the night sky a muted orange up ahead. Flashing red lights brighten the dark and lead our way.

"Get ready, boys," I say, turning to look back at the crew. "Looks like we've got a big one on our hands."

Luca slows and brings the engine to a stop at the cordon surrounding the old warehouse building now raging with flames three-stories high. "Let's go. I'll check in with Cap and give orders after that. We're not first here," I say, looking around to see our 'rivals' Firehouse 22 on scene. Their engine lieutenant Nick Pierce is a grade-A asshole, and he doesn't seem to hide that fact. I really hate deferring to that jerk at a call-out. "It's not our scene to control but just get ready to go in if needed. Yeah?"

"Yes, boss," fills the cab, then we all jump into action.

Hours later, I get back to my soggy Portillo's sandwich.

That's not to say I don't inhale it like it was my last meal on earth.

It's a little bright spot on an otherwise heartbreaking night. Sometimes you've just gotta focus on the good to outweigh the bad.

———

I blame peer pressure.

Not really. After that terrible fire last night, where the bodies of two squatters were found inside, the entire crew needs a big blow-out. And since most of them were already conned into tagging along by Scotty, I won't pass up the opportunity to let off a bit of steam. Scotty is good at a lot of things even though he might not seem it, but charming his way into a woman's heart—or pants—is not his strong suit.

I've been to many bars and clubs over the years, but this is the first time I've been to ladies' night at Throb. I can see why Scotty wanted to come here. In fact, I would hazard a guess that this isn't the first time he's been here for this monthly event.

Earlier in the night, the entire crew was here. After a few hours, my friend Zach left to get back home to his wife and kids, along with a few of the others with families. Now, it's just Rhodes, Luca, Gio, Skye, Cohen and myself, all standing around two tall tables lining the wall of the dance floor. In front of us, Scotty is moving from one potential victim to the next, introducing himself and trying to get some action. It's comical.

"I can't watch anymore," Rhodes mutters, snorting and shaking his head. "It's just too sad." He lifts his chin my way. "Some wingman you are. Aren't you supposed to be helping the dude get laid?"

My lips tip up into a smile. "*You, I* could help. Him?" I ask, looking back just in time to see Scotty getting a martini thrown in his face. "Nope. There's absolutely no chance."

Skye leans into my side and puts her hand on my arm. "Don't look now, but your little realtor is in Scotty's crosshairs."

My head snaps up and I scan the room for the errant horn dog and his prey. Then I catch sight of her and her blonde friend being accosted by Scotty at a table on the edge of the dancefloor.

I put my beer down on the table and push off the wall. "I'll be back. It seems wingmen need to stage rescue missions too."

"For him or for her?" Gio calls out with a laugh.

I grin. "Him, definitely him. He's gonna get eaten alive."

"Maybe they'll eat you instead," Skye says.

"Or castrate the two of you. They kind of look like bad asses," Luca muses.

"It might do the women of Chicago a favor if they put Scotty out to pasture," Rhodes mutters.

"Play nice, Rhodes," I say, but there's absolutely no malice in it.

He holds one hand up in the air. "Hey. I'm just saying what we're all thinking."

"Hold that thought until I get back." I slowly maneuver my way through writhing bodies on the dance floor to the other side of the bar where Renee and her friend are glaring daggers at a seemingly clueless Scotty, who has his hands on his hips and a drunken sway going on.

"Ladies. There's more than enough of the Scottmeister to go around," he slurs.

"God, no. Scotty," I say, wrapping an arm around his shoulders, putting him out of his misery because when a guy is so drunk he talks about himself in the third person, that's when a man who is any friend at all needs to step in. "There's no one right now who wants a piece of the Scottmeister. You're drunk, and your beer goggles are definitely leading you down a path you don't want to travel."

I lock eyes with Renee, the spark of heat I see there making me stand a little straighter and smile a little brighter. *Good to know I wasn't imagining things the other day.*

"Beautiful laaaaaddddiiiieeeessss, have you met my boss man? He's my lieutennnnant. The big cheese," he says, puffing his chest up, making me laugh.

Renee's long, inky hair is swept to one side over her shoulder. Her gleaming white teeth bite into her perfectly shaped ruby-painted lips as her gaze roams down my body and back up again. Tonight, she's wearing a sexy-as-hell dark lace top and skin-tight pants that cling to her curves in a way to entice and tease—something she's achieving with ease.

"Lieutenant?" her blond friend asks with a giggle, turning her head to the brunette goddess I can't look away from. "It's our lucky night, Renee. Two for the price of one."

Renee rolls her eyes. "Hayley. It might pay to lay off the cocktails."

Hayley throws her head back and laughs. "God, Ren. Live a little," she says, throwing her arm around Renee's shoulders, drawing my attention to the enticing smooth skin of Renee's exposed chest. "The least you can do is *try* to enjoy yourself. Look here," she says, nodding my way. "This big, buff *boss* looks right up your alley."

My lips twitch at Hayley because a) she is definitely well on her way to being drunk and should probably switch to water soon, and b) what I wouldn't give to see Renee relax and give me an in. I'm just as mesmerized by her as I was the first time I saw her, after we crashed to the ground with her on top of me.

Renee shakes her head and turns her attention back to me. Her expression goes from "yes, I'm open for business" to "cautious and suspicious" in the blink of an eye. What caused the sudden change? "So . . . Mr. Rossi. Caught any *other* realtors this week?"

"Haven't had much time. I've been too busy working and wondering if my damsel in distress might call," I say with a half smirk, hoping a little charm might get us back on track. It doesn't.

"Working as a lieutenant?" she asks.

"Yes . . ." I say cautiously, sensing a sharp edge in her tone.

"Where?"

Scotty inserts himself back into the conversation, breaking our confusing face-off. "Marco here is my boss. We're firefighters at Firehouse 101."

"Is that so?" Renee says, crossing her arms over her ample chest, instinctively drawing my eyes there. Her body language tells me we've now moved on from cautious and shot straight to dead and buried.

"My sister doesn't like firefighters," Blondie announces, sounding a little disappointed at that fact. "Bad past with—"

"Hayley . . ." Renee warns, but Hayley is too far gone. Her lips tip up into a lopsided grin as she steps forward and loops arms with Scotty. "But that just means more for me." She looks between the two of us and waggles her brows suggestively. "I'm always up for some fun."

"And then I lost her . . ." Renee murmurs with a resigned sigh, and I have to agree with her.

Scotty has never been one to shy away from fire bunnies, and when he straightens and steps out of my hold to move close to Hayley, I know *he* knows he's snagged himself a live one.

"So," Scotty says, slinging his arm around Hayley's shoulders and grinning down at her. "Does my fire bunny wanna dance?"

I groan, my head dropping back and my eyes going to the roof. His line seems to work though, 'cause Hayley nods and buries a giggle into Scotty's chest.

Renee reaches for her sister's arm, brows knitted together, but Hayley just grins at her while Scotty nuzzles her neck. "I'm just gonna go . . . over there, Ren" she announces, melting into my drunk friend. Hayley looks between Renee and I, and flails her arm in the air, gesturing between us. "You two should get acquainted. You know . . ." She leans in, not being subtle. "See what pops up."

Renee grimaces and shakes her head with absolutely no amusement there at all. *Wow. I wonder who shat in her Wheaties.* I'm rethinking my first read on the woman.

"Hayls, remember the rule. Text me if you're going to leave."

Blondie turns and grins at her sister. "Yes, *Mom.*"

We turn and watch Hayley and Scotty stagger onto the dance floor, both of them laughing and hanging off each other. There's absolutely no doubt in my mind that those two are a sure thing for the night. There was a time years ago when that would have been my main goal when going out to a club too. Nowadays, not so much. I'm definitely a quality-over-quantity kind of guy. That comes with age and experience, I guess.

"Should we be worried about those two?" I ask, trying to break the icy aura now surrounding this brunette goddess.

"She's fine. Your *friend* seems harmless. Hayley is big enough to make her own choices, however misguided they might be." Her tone is flatter than the Indiana plains, and there's no doubt in my mind that any interest she felt for me has waned. But my mama didn't raise a quitter, and I've always been a fan of mysteries. I never give up until that last piece is in place and the riddle is solved.

"So . . ." I look down to the ground and spot the same silver heels she was wearing a week ago when we first met. "Fallen into any buyer's arms lately?"

I'm aiming for a lip twitch but get a clenched jaw instead.

I've never seen such disdain shown for my profession before. Not an obvious one, anyway.

I study her while her attention is on her dancing sister, looking for any sign at all that there's a way to get the night back on course. I'm not quite ready to give up on her yet.

"Have you been to ladies' night before?" I ask, trying to scale the wall she's surrounded herself with.

"Hmm?" she asks, absentmindedly, not even flicking a glance my way.

"Do you come here often?" I say without thinking. *Oh shit, talk about cliché.* I open my mouth to take it back, but she beats me to it.

Her narrowed eyes snap to mine. "Seriously?"

I try to muster up some charm in the beautiful face of animosity. "What I mean is, I haven't seen you here before." *That* earns a new quirked brow. *She's totally not going to make this easy for me. She's a challenge, and I'm hooked on figuring her out.*

"Do *you* come to ladies' night and try to use your big muscles and suave moves often? Or maybe you just say 'I'm a firefighter; I've got a big hose and I know how to use it' and wait for women to swoon and fall at your feet?"

My lips curve into an amused smirk. "Would it work on you? Because my next move is to take them to the firehouse and show them my big truck. Then, if they're really good, I'll let them slide down my *long* fireman's pole."

Her eyes widen, and I don't miss the slight quirk of her lips. The fact I'm going toe-to-toe with her seems to have surprised her. It also makes me want to do it again and again.

"Just so you know, I came tonight with my crew because we had a hard night last night. It just *coincided* with ladies' night and some of them were coming anyway. I know the owner, so yes, I've been here a few times before, but I've never seen the ice queen in the corner shooting daggers at me all because she thinks I'm a player without any good reason," I reply.

"I'm sorry, but your friend is currently pawing all over my sister. I'm not sure the good-guy, knight-in-shining-armor routine you've got going on is gonna fly if *that*"—she points over to where Scotty is indeed acting like an octopus with Hayley—"is the kind of guy representing your crew."

"Scotty is one of a kind. He's genuinely harmless, but he is good people."

"And what about you?" she asks curiously, her hazel eyes pinning me in place. God, that look on her face is doing bad, bad, *good* things to me. Something about her sass and attitude is hitting all the right buttons.

"What about me?"

"Are you a player?"

"I don't have time for games."

"Pity," she says dismissively.

I frown, completely confused. "Why?"

"Because then I'd have a reason to throw a drink in someone's face."

I scoff and shake my head. "So you're judging me before getting to know me?"

She turns and faces me dead-on. "Look. I might've been open to the idea, but Hayley is right, I'm not exactly gung-ho when it comes to guys in uniform. It's probably better just to end our night here and now. I'm sure you're a nice guy, Marco, but you might as well quit now and save yourself the trouble." She returns to her perch, leaning into the table and watching the people dancing in front of us. *Why is this woman so damn intriguing to me? I'm like a dog with a bone now.*

"You were interested though. I'm no expert, but you definitely liked what you saw when we met and tonight when I walked over." I sound cocky, but I call things as I see them. That way, there's never any confusion or miscommunication, whatever the situation.

She shrugs, her mouth curving into a half smirk. "There was. You're easy on the eyes, Marco Rossi. I won't deny that. Any red-blooded breathing woman can see that you're hot. But if your 'crew' are all like Scotty, all swagger and 'men about town looking for fresh meat.'" She turns toward me and this time she unabashedly runs hers eyes over my chest, down to my legs and slowly back up again. "It doesn't matter how good you look, or how well you fill those slacks, or how well you can use your *hose*, I'm not interested in being a notch on any firefighter's belt. Been there, done that, lived to tell the tale. Now, if you're going to stay here, can you at least stop trying to charm your way into my pants? That ship has sailed, *Lieutenant,* so save your well-practiced moves for your next target because your aim is well off with me."

I watch the words come out of her mouth, but the shaky resolve I detect underneath them catches my attention. This woman is a fighter, and god dammit, I'm always up for a challenge. Something tells me Renee will make a man fight for his right to stand by her side, but for a woman like her, you know the battle will always be worth it.

There's a spark there. She wouldn't still be trying to justify all the reasons she shouldn't even be interested in me—in the possibility of *us* —if there wasn't. It's almost as if she's trying to convince herself. There's definitely a story there, and I'm more determined than ever to find out what it is.

"Now, if you'll excuse me, I'm just going to the bathroom—I'm telling you this in case Hayley stops sucking face with the *delightful* Scottmeister and wonders where I've gone. If you're still here when I get back, then *maybe* I'll let you explain why you're chatting me up when your wife/girlfriend/whoever she is stands over the other side of the room, grinning at us."

"She's my sister. Did you really think I would flirt with you in front of another woman like that?

"As I said, I have my issues with men in uniform."

Then I see my in. "Yet when you met me, I was out of uniform and saving you from face-planting into the front lawn. And . . ." I step a little closer, not wanting to press my luck, but I do love keeping this woman on her toes. Her breath catches, her chest rising and falling a little faster now. I keep going, dropping my voice to a low whisper for her ears only. "And did you think I'd leave you my phone number, offering to catch you, if I was viewing a house with a significant other?"

She shakes her head and worries her bottom lip between her teeth.

"And would I be here, standing in front of you, asking you out on a date if Skye was anyone but my sister?"

"No . . ." she breathes.

I decide to make a move. It might earn me a slap in the face, or it might just give me one piece of heaven to end this exchange on a high. I close the remaining distance between us, sliding my hand onto her hip and resting it there. When she doesn't push me away, I press on. "So, sweetheart, how about you give me your number and let me call you tomorrow?"

"Hmm," she hums, sounding more than a little dazed. *Fucking beautiful.*

"Renee, will you go out with me?"

She seems to come back into herself. She takes a few steps between us and tilts her head, as if to study me.

"Maybe," she says with a shrug, like I've asked her something bland like, 'How's the weather today?' or 'Do you like pineapple on your pizza?'

"Maybe not," she says, winking at me before she straightens and heads towards the bathroom, leaving me standing there, suddenly alone and absolutely dumbfounded.

That's not to say my eyes aren't glued to her fantastic ass as she struts away.

Damn. That really did just happen. I was in, then she shot me down before I ended up with a maybe. I'm not sure whether to call that a win, loss, or draw.

Renee looks back over her shoulder, her eyes locking with mine. I don't miss her slight smirk And I definitely don't miss the extra swing in her hips as she disappears from sight.

I can't wipe the grin off my face. The irony. She's accused *me* of being a player when she was the one doing the playing all along.

One thing is for sure. That woman just got a lot more interesting. I was already intrigued to begin with, and now more than ever, I can't wait to find out more about the brunette goddess.

I always said I wanted a show stopper.

Something tells me, I may have just found one.

3

RENEE

Today is a big day. Word-of-mouth has me standing in the middle of a high-rise apartment in the Gold Coast neighborhood, being shown around by a woman named Gilly.

"Your place is beautiful, Mrs. Baker."

She waves me off. "Mrs. Baker is my mother-in-law and as much as I love her, it makes me feel a lot older than I already do."

I snort at that, because Gilly doesn't look a day over thirty-five and has a body with curves for days that you can just tell her husband enjoys—especially if her slightly mussed hair is anything to go by.

Her husband, Ezra, shook my hand and introduced himself, then weirdly said Skye had highly recommended me.

It took me a few moments to remember where I'd heard that name before. Skye, sister of Marco. The woman he'd made sure I knew wasn't his wife or girlfriend.

Then Ezra had kissed his wife in a far-from-appropriate fashion, and told me Gilly was the boss and it was her decision.

That was forty minutes ago.

"Sorry. *Gilly*, what do you think about my plan for staging and marketing the property? If you were to proceed, of course." *Please say yes. Mama needs some new Jimmy Choos.*

She studies me for a few seconds. "I'm thinking it's two o'clock, and we definitely need wine," she announces, and my heart stutters for a moment. Then I can't help the half smile that appears. "Will you join me?"

"If it's to celebrate signing with me, then absolutely," I say, jokingly.

She walks into the kitchen and pulls out a chilled bottle of white from the refrigerator, then pulls down two glasses from the overhead cabinet. "Of course it's to celebrate." I do a little jump for joy in my head. "But it's also because my darling mother-in-law has both our two kids tonight, and I'm pre-gaming for a date with my husband."

"Nice," I say approvingly. "A woman after my own heart."

She pours two *very* healthy doses of wine and walks around the kitchen island. She hands one glass to me and nods over to the balcony where there are two big outdoor couches facing the lake. Places like these make me love my job. Hayls would flip if she saw this apartment.

"We love this place. Ezra has had it ever since his second divorce."

Internally, my eyes are bugging out of my head and rolling off the twentieth-floor balcony, but since I'm a professional, I don't outwardly react.

Gilly's eyes dance with amusement. "Oh, you're good," she says with a smirk. "Yes. My darling husband—bless his heart—chose the wrong woman *twice* before getting it right the third time with me. And since I'm the one who gets to keep him now, I'd probably shake the exes' hands if I ever met them." A giggle escapes me. "But now we've got two kids and they need space, and we're pretty well covered with rentals, so this is the first property on the chopping block—so to speak."

"It's beautiful, and I'm not just saying that because I scored the listing," I say with a wry smile. Gilly takes a sip of her wine, her eyes coming my way. "We're actually planning on selling our two-story place in Wicker Park too, if you're interested."

I have to bite my lip to stop my mouth from dropping open. Two listings in one day, and all because I tripped into a sexy man's arms two weeks ago? *What kind of sorcery is this?*

Gilly sits first, and I follow her lead. "So, what do you say about taking on both listings?"

"I'd love to."

"Awesome." She curls her legs up and seems to get comfortable on the couch, as if she's settling in for a while. It's lucky I have nothing else booked for today. "Now, Renee. Since we're in business together. Why don't you tell me all about yourself?" *I guess it's not the strangest thing I've been asked by a client...*

"Okay. I'm thirty-four, and I've lived in Chicago for the past ten years."

Gilly nods for me to continue. *Why is this weird?*

"Um . . . I live with my sister, Hayley, in a two-bed duplex I own near West Garfield Park."

"That's a nice area. Friends of ours have flipped a few houses near there."

Wait. Surely not. "Do you mean Cook Construction?"

Her eyes widen, her expression becoming animated as she bounces in the chair. "Yes. How do you know them?"

"I've sold a few of their houses, actually. They do amazing work."

"That they do," she replies. "My sister married Jax Cook, and Ezra is an honorary Cook brother too."

A surprised laugh escapes my lips. "Wow. Small world then, huh?"

"Definitely." She nods. "Enough of the standard things. Give me something juicy about you."

I scrunch up my face. "Like what?"

"I know," she says, taking a sip of her wine. "If you had three words to describe yourself on a dating profile, what would they be?"

Why are my Spidey senses tingling?

"Does this have anything to do with me signing your listing?"

She smiles. "Oh God, no. And it's *listings,* remember?" She finishes her glass and stands up. "Hold that thought—I'll just go grab the bottle and bring it out here. Ez will come by to get me so I'm not driving. We can always send you home in a car too."

I don't know why, but her reassurance relaxes me. And Gilly seems lovely. Like someone I could be friends with if I didn't work dumb hours all the time. Although, I will say this is the first time I've been subjected to a Spanish Inquisition at a listing appointment before.

Then again, it's a Friday, and I'm on the twentieth-floor balcony of a million-dollar apartment, so can I really complain?

She walks back and does a sneaky top-up of my glass as she walks past. *I definitely like her now.*

"Sorry if it seems like I'm interrogating you. I have two toddlers, so I'm used to drilling them for info for the fastest, most mess-saving response."

I snort. I can totally see that method has merit.

"But I also spend a lot of time with those toddlers, so given the chance for stimulating adult conversation, I go for it."

I wave my hand in the air. "I get that. Go right ahead. Ask me anything. Another glass of wine and I'll be looser than a town bike on payday."

Gilly splutters and cracks up laughing. "You would get along with my sister, Ronnie. She's full of crazy sayings like that too."

I tilt my head and shrug. "Hayley and I have made it a game to try and come up with the most outrageous similes we can. The more shocking and offensive, the better."

"I definitely like you more now," she says. "So, c'mon, tell me. Where were you before Chicago?"

"Milwaukee, born and raised."

"So old Chicago then?" she teases, her lips twitching.

"Ah, spoken like a true Chicago sports fan. Let me guess: Cubs, Bears and Blackhawks till you die?"

"Cubs—yes, 'cause my husband would make me ex-wife number three if I didn't. Bears—nope. I'm actually a Chiefs fan because *hello,* Patrick Mahomes is a god. And hockey?" She scrunches her nose up. "I can take it or leave it but Ezra is a diehard Hawks supporter and will probably wanna be buried in a jersey."

My lips curve up. "So sports is not that big in your house, then?"

"Noooo, not at *all,*" she replies, both of us snickering.

"Okay. To turn the tables, Packers, Bucks, and the Hawks. And Hayley works for the Chicago Fire soccer team, so I get dragged along to those games too."

Gilly's brows lift up. "Interesting. So, what else is there to know about you? Do you have a husband, boyfriend, secret baby daddy somewhere?"

"Nope, nope, and I'd know if I did."

"How? You're hot, you're funny, and you can obviously take care of yourself. Men love a strong, independent woman," she says, looking me up and down.

"You tell me and we'll both know," I say with a grin. "Honestly, I came out of a bad relationship a few years ago, and since then, I've been focused on building up my client list and networking. My mom was a typical stay-at-home housewife who was totally reliant on the man she was with, and I never wanted to find myself in that position. I'm all about equality and trust in a relationship. Without that, what have you got?"

"See? And *this* is another reason I like you. You're strong-minded and won't let a man walk all over you. Take it from someone who rules the roost in her marriage—guys dig it." She leans in. "They *really* dig it."

"Yes, yes we do," Ezra says, appearing out of thin air and wrapping his arms around his wife's shoulders from behind. He looks my way. "Hey, Renee. Looks like my wife has inducted you into her little wine club."

Gilly looks up at her husband and kisses under his jaw. "I'm preparing for date night," she says softly.

Ezra turns and gives her a hard, fast but rather passionate kiss on the lips before straightening. "And Lord knows I approve of *that.*"

I down my glass and stand, smoothing down my skirt as I go. "I better get going."

"Hey, don't leave on my account. I need to do some work anyway."

Gilly looks up at me. "You don't have to go. Ezra is used to hanging around girls. He has two sisters who used to talk his ear off growing up. And besides, we were just getting to the juicy stuff."

Ezra's amused eyes drift down to his wife. The two of them share some unspoken conversation which awakens my Spidey senses again, but I have no idea why. Call it self-protective suspicion. "Sweetheart . . ." he grumbles affectionately.

She holds her hands up in surrender. "What? Just a little recon, that's all."

His lips twitch. "And we said we would stay out of it."

"Stay out of what?"

"A few weeks ago, you met Skye and her brother at a house showing . . ."

The penny drops. Is this Marco's doing? He gave me two listings with *big* potential commissions, all to get me to go out with him?

"Marco?" I ask. Granted, the man does intrigue me, and he has occupied my thoughts a lot since the club—more than I thought he would, anyway. But I'm not sure I'm comfortable with this play.

Gilly's head jerks back. "Oh, God no. Skye—his sister. She's determined to play matchmaker with you two."

"Oh," I say. Didn't see that one coming.

"Her heart's in the right place, and we're not signing with you because of that. Business is separate from our personal lives."

I breathe a sigh of relief. "Thank you for saying that. Now I'm just glad I didn't tell you my deepest, darkest secrets."

"Believe me, even if you had, Gilly wouldn't have shared. She's of the firm belief you have to make a guy work for it," Ezra says with a smirk.

Gilly winks at me. "And look what happens when you do, baby daddy."

The soft smile Ezra shoots his wife is nothing short of dazzling. "Totally worth it."

"I do need to get going. But I'll get my assistant to send you through the draft listing contracts and then we can schedule a coffee next week to sign them?"

Gilly stands, putting her glass down as she does. She holds her hand out to me to shake. Ezra does the same, then she leads me back into the apartment and toward the front door.

"I hope you didn't mind the twenty questions," she says cautiously.

"Not at all. It makes sense now. Besides, it was more like five, not twenty."

"I was gearing up for some juicy ones, I swear."

I laugh at that. "Maybe next time. But maybe you can even the score by telling me something about Marco. A girl's gotta have some ammunition under her belt." Especially if I'm going to keep crossing paths with the man.

She opens the door and taps her chin. "Hmm. He's the oldest of five, Skye being the baby. She's a paramedic. The others are a fire-fighter, a cop, and an aesthetician. They're Chicago born and bred, and his mama makes amazing gnocchi."

"Damn."

"What?"

"I'm a sucker for a good gnocchi," I say.

"You're perfect for a Rossi man. Those boys have been tearing up the female population of Chicago for years, by all accounts."

My face falls and Gilly doesn't miss it.

"No, no. Not terribly. I mean . . . shit. You'd think, being a lawyer, I'd learn not to put my foot in my mouth."

"Hey. All the lawyers I've ever known have a tendency to do that occasionally," I reply, trying to break the weird change in atmosphere.

"I just know that men like that, with high-stress jobs and lots of testosterone around them, like to blow off steam. Skye holds her brothers in very high regard, though. She even held off hooking up with her now husband because they all work together, and those brothers are super-protective."

Now *that* I'd believe. "Okay, tell me this and I'll let you report back to Skye anything and everything I said."

Gilly nods, fighting a grin. There's no missing the fact she's all in on this matchmaking malarkey. "Hit me with it and if I know, I'll share."

"Is he single now?"

Her head jerks back. "There's no way we'd set any woman up for a fall, and there's also no way any of the men in our lives—husbands, brothers, or otherwise—would ever cheat on a woman. They're honest to a fault, protective as hell, and, the most fun part . . . they're dedicated to the chase when they find the one they want."

"Hmm. Good to know. Then report back to Skye and tell her whatever you want. But if Marco wants me, then I'm all about being the chasee. If he wants the water, he's going to have to come to the well and dip the bucket in."

We leave it at that, but my entire way home I totally overthink my decision. Then I decide, fuck it; Gilly has nothing to gain by playing up what a good guy Marco might be. Maybe it's time I find out for myself.

Once he makes the first move though. What kind of chasee would I be otherwise?

4

MARCO

Sunday afternoon and I'm walking into my parents' house, feeling tired from my last twenty-four-hour shift.

"Mama?" I call out.

"In here, Marco," my mother replies from halfway down the hall.

In the kitchen, I find Mama, Skye, Cohen, and Valentina seated at stools around the center island.

After greeting the girls with a kiss on the cheek and Co with a handshake, I move around to my mother and pull her in for a big hug.

"It's good to see you, son." She shifts back and looks in my eyes. "You look tired though. You work too hard."

I smile down at her and shake my head. "You say that to all of us."

"A mother never stops worrying about her children. You know that, Marco Rossi."

"Except me. I *never* look tired," Val says, glowing like she's slept for twenty hours.

"That's the beauty of cosmetics," Skye muses, earning a gasp.

Val leans over and points her finger at her. "Take that back, brat!"

That just makes Skye smirk. "If the concealer fits."

"Bit—"

"Valentina Maria," Mama growls in a scary 'don't mess with me' tone, just as Luca and Gio walk in together, followed by Papa.

"Who's in trouble?" Luca says with a singsong voice.

"Val," Skye, Co, and I say in unison, making everyone except Mama and Val chuckle.

"It's always Val," Gio says, walking over to said sister and ruffling her hair in the way we know she hates.

"Be nice to my girl," my father says, moving to Mama and kissing her temple.

"Val or Mama?" I ask with a half grin.

"Mama, of course. Always your mother, till the day I take my last breath." He's whispering by the end, earning a soft look from his wife.

This is why I've held out for a show stopper. A woman worth anything life throws at you and then some. *That's* why I'm almost thirty-nine and single, working up to three twenty-four-hour shifts a week, and living in a house with Gio. Luca *used* to live with us, but working and living together was a bit too much for both of us to cope with.

Speaking of brothers . . . "Hey, where did you guys get to this morning?" I ask, switching between Gio and Luca.

"We went for a run along the Lakefront Trail."

"You went for a run after your shift?" I ask Luca.

"Yep. Like it's hard," he says.

Skye snorts. "You guys are crazy."

Luca lifts his shirt and twists his shoulders from side to side, flexing his abs. "Gotta keep in shape for the ladies."

"Oh God," Val groans. I just drop my head and chuckle, as does Dad.

"And on *that* note, why don't you all help me carry these plates through to the dining table so we can eat," Mama says.

A chorus of, "Yes, Mama" follows. I pick up a plate and my siblings follow, obeying Mama as we always do. With five out of the six of us doing shift work—and not always following the same schedule—we make sure to all get together for these meals so we can connect as a family.

We're all very close, so it's something we never miss.

Once we're seated, Papa stands and says grace before we dig in and dish up our plates.

"I heard you guys caught a big one last night?" Gio says, looking over at Luca and myself.

I nod. "Yeah. House fire in a three-flat. Took most of the night to get under control."

Papa arches a brow. "Arson?"

"Seems that way. We found evidence of an incendiary device, but the investigators will know more once they can get in there."

"Did everyone get out?" Gio asks.

"Everyone that we knew about, yep."

Mama does the sign of the cross, making me smile. "Thank heavens."

"Are we all set for Marco's birthday dinner next weekend? I've made the booking for seven p.m. and it's the first day Luca and Marco are off-shift, which gives you two time to sleep," Mama says, her soft blue eyes drifting around the table.

"Sounds good, Mama," I say with a smile. "I'm looking forward to it."

"And you chose Japanese this year. That's exciting," she says, almost looking excited at the prospect of a teppanyaki dinner.

"And will you be bringing a date?" Mama asks, waggling her eyebrows at me, and I almost laugh.

I shoot her my best adoring son expression. "You know you're the only woman in my life, Mama," I say, earning groans from everyone except Mama, who sighs, and my father, who chuckles.

"So, Val. How's online dating going?" Skye asks. There's no missing the twinkle in her eye and I know she's trying to stitch our sister up.

"It's fine . . ." Val answers, drawing out the words.

"And your date on Friday night?" *The little brat is in fine form today.*

"Oh, Valentina. You didn't tell me you were seeing someone," Mama says, jumping all over this conversation—just like Skye intended.

If looks could kill, Skye would be seriously injured by now as Val's eyes cut through her.

Her expression is all business when she looks down the table at our mother. "We've only been out a few times. We're still getting to know each other," she replies, rather diplomatically.

"But he must be a good man to catch the eye of our daughter. You wouldn't give someone the time of day unless he was worth your time," Mama says.

Val's cheeks turn pink and she studies the green salad on her plate. "He's okay."

I glance across to Gio, Skye and Cohen, sitting opposite me, and note they're all either smiling or quietly laughing.

Unfortunately, that's when Skye moves on to her next target—me.

"Marco, I forgot to tell you. We saw Gilly and Ezra yesterday, and they've signed both the apartment and their house with your favorite realtor."

My head snaps up before I can catch my reaction. "What?"

Val leans forward in her chair and turns my way. She's probably just happy the spotlight has shifted onto me. *Just my luck.* "Now, *this* sounds far more interesting. Who's Marco's *realtor?*"

I go to say something but Skye beats me to it. "So two weeks ago, I asked Marco to come with me to look at a house I'd seen for sale that I thought Co and his brothers could flip."

"Okay . . . but that's doesn't explain why she's *Marco's* realtor. Are you planning on selling?" Val asks, adorably clueless as always.

Luca snorts beside me, earning a quick elbow jab in return. "Ouch. Motherfu—"

I turn and glare at him and he wisely shuts up.

"Renee's *his* realtor because Marco here has taken a bit of a liking to her in the two times we've seen her," Skye says, leaning back in her chair and grinning like the Cheshire cat.

"Twice?" Mama asks, her gaze firmly locked on me.

"We ran into her when we went out for drinks last weekend," I reply. Skye—still in the mood to drop me in it—keeps going.

"We went to Throb for crew drinks. You know, the nightclub that's also a—"

"It was ladies' night, Mama. We went to relax after a tough week and also support Scotty," Luca says.

That earns snickers from us kids since that's a very diplomatic way of putting it.

"Hang on," I say with a frown. "How did Gilly and Ez know about Renee?"

"Renee's a nice name," Mama murmurs, and I try not to throw a potato at Skye's head.

Skye doesn't answer and by the apologetic look Cohen's sending me, I know I'm not gonna like this.

"Skye . . ." I grumble, low and menacing.

Her guilty eyes meet mine. "I just thought I'd recommend her. She was really nice, and you guys seemed to get along well so I . . .

put in a good word for her with Gilly and Ez, and then Gilly might have—"

"Matchmaker Skye strikes again," Luca muses under his breath. She looks away but I'm not in the mood to let this go.

"What did you do, Skye?"

"We just wanted to make sure she was good enough for you," she blurts out.

"You don't think it's up to *me* to determine that?"

Skye's eyes flash and I know it's on like Donkey Kong now. "And what were you doing about it, Marco? Huh? Have you got her phone number? Have you asked her out? Maybe made your interest known? Because we could all see you were both into each other at the club, and you still ended up coming back to our table . . . *alone*."

"Brat, my love life is exactly that. *Mine*."

"Aha. See? You *do* like her," Skye shouts, jumping to her feet. "I *knew* it."

I can't help but smile at that. Everyone else around the table laughs.

"So, little sister. What *did* Gilly find out about Marco's realtor?" Val asks, leaning forward.

"She's from Milwaukee, and—"

"Stop. I don't wanna hear this from you," I say, softening my voice. "If I wanna find out things about her, I'll ask her myself."

"I was just trying to help," Skye says, batting her lashes and looking at me with her big blue eyes that she knows have done a number on me since she was born.

"I know," I say, my lips twitching. "But does she *know* that you recommended her and probably put Gilly up to interrogating her?"

Skye grimaces. "She guessed."

Of course she did. She's not an idiot.

"And when was this?"

"Friday."

I groan. "Shit, Skye."

"Language, son," Papa says.

"Sorry, Mama," I say, looking down the table at her before returning my eyes to my baby sister. "I guess now I *will* have to message her to apologize."

"Or you could just ask her out," Cohen says. "She's not hard on the eye, Mar."

Skye shrugs. She's not one of those women who scolds her husband for stating the obvious—and Cohen knows it.

"Send her flowers," Mama suggests. "Women love surprise flowers."

Valentina shakes her head. "Mama, I love you, but flowers from a man you've met twice and haven't gone on a date with, let alone given your address and/or phone number to? Nope. That's just a little stalkerish."

Luca frowns. "Then how is he supposed to apologize?"

"He doesn't," Val says with a shrug, looking my way. "You don't apologize for your baby sister wanting the best for you. Just tell her the truth and roll with it."

"Well, huh," Gio says, sounding just as surprised as I am, because that's exactly what I was going to do when I got home.

Skye nods in agreement. "Gilly answered her question about you too."

My head snaps to Skye. "She asked about me?"

Mama giggles. "Ah. Good call, Skye. My Marco *is* interested in her." A low hum of amusement goes around the table.

"She asked whether you were single. Gilly made sure Renee knew you were a good guy," Skye replies, answering my unasked question.

"Well, of course he is. He's a Rossi," my dad says, leaning over and patting my shoulder. "Any woman would be lucky to get a Rossi man."

That earns a proud smile from Mama, giggles from the girls, and amused headshakes from the boys.

Whereas me, I just groan. *Lord help me.*

My only hope now is that Renee is the understanding, give-me-another-chance type of woman.

Then again, I've never been one to shy away from a challenge.

Which is probably why later Sunday night, I'm sitting in my leather recliner, the Cubs playing a game on the West Coast on the TV in front of me, and my phone is in my hand. Renee's number is on the screen after I looked it up online.

Since Gio is working, I can't ask him whether to send a text message or call her, so I decide Rhodes is the best person to give advice.

He was married for fifteen years to his high school sweetheart. Lily tragically passed away from ovarian cancer five years ago. That left Rhodes as a single dad to a now fifteen-year-old son. He's one of the smartest, most loyal, and selfless men I know, and one of my closest friends.

"Hey," he says.

"Hey. You free to talk?"

"Is the Pope a Catholic?"

"And is Scotty the idiot who actually had to stop and think about that one?"

"You know it." He laughs. "But yeah, you're all good. Jake and I are just chilling on the couch watching *Days of Thunder.*"

"Kicking back old school, then?"

"Every guy needs to see Tom Cruise in his heyday."

"Truer words have never been spoken."

When comfortable silence falls between us, it's not long till Rhodes gets straight to it. "C'mon. Spill."

"So this is gonna sound totally lame but should I text Renee or call her?"

"Wait. Renee? The realtor? I thought you didn't get her number," he says.

"Ah, yeah . . . well, the brat decided to play matchmaker and do some undercover reconnaissance and got Gilly to secretly interrogate her but wasn't very good at it. Now Renee knows Skye was meddling, and I know Skye meddled. So I looked up her number."

"You were going to call her anyway."

"I was. This week. I was going to turn up at one of her listings and ask her out again, and this time make sure I get a yes."

"Text her, Uncle Marco!" Jake yells out in the background. "It won't freak her out as much. It won't be as awkward as an unsolicited phone call either. Just don't send a dick pic as a conversation starter; you might not get the answer you're hoping for."

Then both father and son crack up laughing, as do I.

"So now I have a fifteen-year-old schooling me on dating," I say with a grin.

Rhodes chuckles. "Hey. If I ever decide to date, I'll probably be asking Jake for advice too."

"Ha ha, Dad. You, date!" Then Jake's uncontrollable laughter filters down the line again.

"Smart kid," I muse.

"Yeah. Sometimes he's *too* smart."

I smile at that. Rhodes has done an amazing job with that kid. It's been those two against the world, with help from Rhodes' parents so he could still work and support Jake. Everyone from the firehouse chipped in whenever and wherever they could, but any less of a man might've let their world crumble around them. Rhodes has stayed strong—in public anyway.

"I better go so you guys can finish your movie."

"And you go google the lovely Renee and somehow explain why your baby sister felt the need to play matchmaker."

Yeah, there's that too.

"Got her number. Now I just need to send the message."

"Go for casual. Might give you half a chance before she blocks your number," Rhodes says, snickering.

"Thanks, *friend*."

"Anytime, Marky Mark. Come around tomorrow for dinner. Jake's cooking some fancy thing he learned on YouTube."

"Is that code for 'come save me from being poisoned' or what?"

"It's code for 'come over and have your taste buds dazzled!'"

"Tell Jake it's a date," I say.

"Bye, and good luck. If a woman has you this interested after only a chance encounter or two, you're screwed."

"Probably, but isn't that half the fun?"

Rhodes chuckles. "You're not wrong there."

"You two have a good night," I say before ending the call.

Then I bring up Renee's number, take a deep breath, and type out my message.

Marco – It appears I have a sister who likes to interrogate women I'd like to date, and she didn't even report back with any useful intel.

Not a minute later, my phone vibrates with a reply.

Renee – It took you long enough, Lieutenant.

Marco – Does this mean you'll go out with me?

Renee – Never picked you for a quick draw, Mr. Rossi. Don't disappoint me before we've even begun.

Marco –That's not a no . . .

Renee – It's not a yes yet either . . .

5

RENEE

Monday

Marco – Hey. How's your day going? Fallen into the arms of any men lately?

Renee – Good afternoon, Lieutenant. I've had no showings today. I'm in the office proofing marketing materials and doing boring admin stuff. Unless I trip over my own feet and my fifty-five-year-old broker John catches me, I don't think I'll be needing your rescue services today.

Marco – I wouldn't rule it out. So, what heels are you wearing?

Renee – Should I take that question as you admitting to a foot fetish?

Marco – Isn't it a little early in our relationship to be asking about sexual preferences?

Renee – Isn't it a little presumptuous to be using labels?

Marco – Touché.

Renee – Don't think I didn't notice you didn't answer my question, Lieutenant.

Wednesday

Marco – My sister just told me you're a closet Brewers fan. Please tell me she's screwing with me, otherwise it might be the first thing in your con column.

Renee – Brewers . . . they're a football team, right?

Marco – On my way to a call-out now, but don't think I'm going to let this one go.

Renee – No, definitely not a Brewers fan. Cubs for life, through and through. I fly the W proudly. Be safe, Lieutenant.

Marco – Always, princess.

Renee – Princess. . . I like it.

Marco – Just say the word and I'll bow down at your feet willingly.

Thursday

Renee – Lieutenant Rossi, I've heard you are a good guy. Do you have further testimonials to support this claim?

Marco – You sure know how to make a long shift go faster. And no, I don't have a collection of references to hand out to future dates.

Renee – That is a shame. Word-of-mouth is key in my line of work.

Marco – Surely my meddling sister's confirmation that I'm not a douchebag is proof enough?

Renee – LOL. Skye might just see you as a charity case that needs a woman's touch.

Marco – I'm trying so hard not to go near that one. I will say that I'm not afraid to put in the work to get a woman's touch on my own.

Renee – I'll put that in your pro column then.

Marco – I hope you've got a lot of room on that side of the list. You're going to need it.

Friday

Marco – Roses are red, Violets are blue, all I want for my birthday tomorrow, is the promise of a date with you.

Renee – LMAO are you serious?

Marco – I may be a little buzzed, but I'm an honest drunk.

Renee – And you thought texting me while intoxicated would convince me to accept the date you haven't asked me out on yet?

Marco – What would your answer be if I did?

Renee – It's still a maybe . . . is it really your birthday tomorrow?

Marco – Yup. Thirty-nine and never been kissed.

Renee – Now THAT I find hard to believe. I thought you were an honest drunk?

Marco – I'd be honest if you were here with me now.

Renee – And where is here?

Marco – My house. Us guys are just having a couple of quiet drinks. What are you up to?

Renee – Saying my prayers and reading the bible.

Marco – What are you praying for? I'm already yours for the taking.

Renee – You're also a funny drunk. Is your delightful friend Scotty there?

Marco – The Scottmeister is in fine form tonight.

Renee – So should I warn my sister she might be getting a booty call again?

Marco – Wait . . . AGAIN? They actually hooked up?

Renee – Yep. I woke up the morning after the club to find a half-naked Scotty sitting in my kitchen.

Marco – I'm so sorry. No one wants to see that first thing in the morning.

Renee – That's what Hayley said after he left.

Marco – In his defense, he is a good guy. He's just a little . . .

Renee – Clueless when it comes to women?

Marco – BINGO. Anyway, I'll leave you to your conversations with God.

Marco – Any other plans for the weekend?

Renee – I'm doing my sister a favor and having dinner with a new soccer player who's just been signed to the team.

Renee – Marco? You still with me?

Marco – Dinner? Or a blind date?

Renee – Is it blind if I've seen a photo?

Marco – Is it cheating if you're already planning on going out on a date with a handsome and charming firefighter you met?

Renee – Is it planning if the handsome and charming firefighter hasn't asked me out on a date again yet?

Marco – You forgot to say sexy firefighter . . .

Renee – Goodnight, Marco. Happy birthday for tomorrow. Make a wish when you blow out your candles.

Marco – There's only one thing I want, princess.

Renee – Then all you have to do is ask when you're sober.

Marco – Watch this space.

The next night, I'm led into the restaurant by Antoine Laurent. I chant to myself. It's just a friendly dinner. It's *just* a friendly dinner. If Hayley hadn't begged me to go through with it, promising to make it up to me and telling me it'll help her cred at work, I wouldn't still be here.

That's because my soccer-playing dinner companion has been trying to touch me every chance he's gotten since he picked me up from home in his Italian sports car, one hour late.

I've never been a fan of showy guys, or men who feel the need to overcompensate for what women can tell are their obvious shortcomings. In Antoine's case, it's a personality, the ability to talk about anything or anyone other than himself, and, judging by the overwhelming volume of cologne he's wearing, his half-undone shirt, the ostentatious gold watch on his wrist and the slimy smile he sent the hostess when we arrived, there's a reason he has to be set up for 'dinners' like this one. To put it bluntly, he has absolutely no chance without a little help.

I already knew I wasn't a fan of men in uniform—I can thank my philandering ex and his addiction to fire bunnies for that—but so far, my time with Antoine has me scratching sportsmen off the list too.

We sit in awkward silence, me looking around the semi-full restaurant and admiring the very zen decor, while Antoine leans back in his chair, man-spreading his legs under the table so far I can barely escape, yet he seems far more engrossed with the phone in his hand than initiating friendly conversation. I take the chance to quickly send Hayley a text.

Renee – You owe me BIG TIME for this.

Hayley – Aww. Is he really that bad?

Renee – You should be here instead of me.

Hayley – Well first, there's a fraternization policy and second, you don't put up with bullshit. And Antoine can be a little . . .difficult

Renee – NOW you tell me. I'm not sure even I can suffer this fool.

I slip my phone back into my purse and decide to at least make an effort at making conversation. I didn't get my hair done, shave my legs, buy new shoes, and get dressed up just to talk to myself all night —okay, maybe the shoes *are* for me.

"So, how are you finding Chicago so far?" I ask.

He looks up, his half-lidded gaze roaming down to my chest then slowly back to my eyes. I have to fight my body's instinctive shudder.

"I'm enjoying the sights, that's for sure," he croons. *Um, eww!*

Thankfully, the waitress appears to take our order.

"Hi. I'm Holly and I'm your waitress for this evening. Unfortunately, because it's getting late, our chef's specials have sold out, but everything else on our menu is available."

"Thank you. Can I please have—"

"We'll have a bottle of your most expensive red wine, and we'll have two of the best of everything," Antoine says, speaking over me and looking at the waitress like she's no better than the dirt on the bottom of his Salvatore Ferragamo loafers. Holly's mouth drops open slightly but she catches it and plasters a professional expression on her face.

She turns my way, and I shoot her a sympathetic 'I feel you' smile. "And would you like to—"

"I've ordered for her. That will be all," my *date* says, making it clear he's dismissing her.

"Yes, Mr. Laurent," she says. I mouth a quick, *"I'm sorry,"* which earns me a sympathetic nod before she moves away.

If he keeps this up, allegiance to my sister or not, he'll be eating alone and I'll gladly Uber home and order in. Life's too short for egotistical assholes who think they're God's gift to the women of Chicago. I don't care how many zeros there are in his bank account. An asshole is an asshole, no matter what.

"That was rude, Antoine," I say.

"What was rude?" he replies flippantly, placing his phone face down on the table between us.

I quirk a brow. "Do you want a list?"

He dares to grin at me. "Okay, Renee. What's on the list?"

"You ordered for me without asking. You—"

"Chicks love that shit."

I jerk back, my eyes jumping out as if they're making a run for it. "I can confirm that *chicks* do not love that 'shit,' as you so eloquently put it."

He tilts his head, his eyes narrowing as if to study me. "Ah, you're one of those feminist types."

One of those—

"You know, the women who like to stand their ground and exert their independence when really, they still get wet when a man pays for them, showers them with expensive gifts and . . ." He waves his hand in the air and looks around the room. ". . . takes them to expensive restaurants."

With every word out of his slimy, douche-faced lips, my mouth drops wider open. *Did he just . . . did I hear him correctly?*

Holly returns with the bottle of red wine that I am determined to drink in its entirety—purely to survive this damn date.

"Thank you," I murmur, shooting her a grateful smile. I lift the glass to my lips and take a slow, measured sip when he makes his move, his palm sliding over my knee, his fingers resting on the inside of my leg.

I quickly jerk it away, not missing the amused twitch of his lips. He's testing the waters and weirdly, it's almost as if he gets off on pushing the limits. *No surprise there. He's probably not used to women with a backbone.*

My purse vibrates next to my foot. Since this is more like a blind favor my sister is going to owe me for—for a *long*, long time—I don't think twice before muttering, "Excuse me," and leaning down to grab my phone from my bag.

When I straighten and side-glance at my date, I catch his eyes firmly glued to my ass. When I arch my brow at him, he has the balls to smirk. I think Antoine needs a new name—Douche Canoe seems to be a good fit.

As far as I'm concerned, the sooner we can finish our meal and get out of here, the better. You can bet I'm going to eat the food he ordered for me. I mean, I *shaved* for this. I deserve to at least get fed for my pain and suffering.

Before I can read the first message, another one comes through. I can't help my lips curving up at seeing Marco's name on the screen.

Marco – Of all the restaurants in Chicago.

My entire body goes as frozen as the lake in winter. My head snaps up and I look around the room, but I can't see him anywhere.

Then I read the next message.

Marco – And I can tell you'd much rather be on a date with me. Your body language is so frigid right now, I might start calling you Alaska.

I don't even think about Antoine before typing out my reply. All I want to know is where Marco Rossi is, and how he can see me when I can't see him.

Renee – Ah, it's the birthday boy. BTW, I'm starting to wonder if you ARE stalking me. Where are you?

Marco – Is it stalking if the stalkee is willing?

Renee – Surely it can't be a coincidence when you keep crossing paths with the same person over and over again?

Marco – I call it fortunate serendipity.

Renee – Or stalking . . . where are you?

Marco – Look to the right of the front door at the entry to the teppanyaki bar.

I lift my chin and slowly follow his directions, then lock eyes with his warm melted chocolate ones. My gaze dips to his perfectly curved mouth tipping up on one side. *God, a mouth like that should be outlawed.*

Marco – Uh-oh. Don't look now. Seems your date has realized he's not the sun in your solar system and he doesn't look happy about it.

I snort, not giving two hoots whether he's happy or not. I'm waiting for the ostentatious food he ordered for me, eating it, then I'm out.

Renee – Honestly, there's no room in his galaxy for anything but his ego.

Marco – Need an escape plan? You know I have a thing about saving damsels in distress.

That one makes my lips tip up in a smile.

Renee – I haven't even gotten anything good out of this dinner. The appetizers HE ordered for me are due any minute.

Marco – What if I promise to feed you?

I glance up to find his attention squarely focused on me. It's as if the other patrons mulling around us fade away, leaving just the two of us.

My mouth waters and I'm not sure whether it's from the promise of food or the man who's staring across a crowded restaurant at me.

Renee – I should probably see this through.

Marco – Well, the offer is there if you need it.

I grin as a warm feeling fills me up.

Renee – Thank you, Lieutenant. You truly do live to serve.

Marco – Oh you have no idea, princess.

It's probably best to put my phone down and at least try to return my attention back to my dinner companion.

Except the look he's giving me tells me Marco was right in his deduction that my date is far from impressed with my lack of attention.

He nods at my phone. "You're smiling more at your phone than you have the entire time you've been with me."

I bite my tongue to stop the retort begging to pass my lips. "Sorry." I slip the offending electronic device back into my purse. I lift a brow. "You were saying?"

He moves his knee and his hand at the same time in a sneak attack. *Man, the balls on this guy!* I reach down, grab hold of his thumb, and jerk it back in a little move I learned from self-defense classes at college. He squeals like a pig and snatches his arm back at the same time as the waitress appears at our table with our appetizers. Not a second later, Marco looms over me, his angry eyes stabbing into my asshole date.

"You touched her," he growls and for a woman who doesn't pander to peacocking alpha-males, the gravelly tone of Marco's voice touches me in a way I haven't experienced in a long, *long* time.

I catch the waitress's telling smirk as she slides the plates onto the table and quickly steps away. I dart to my feet and put my palm on Marco's chest. Now that he's here, maybe we should have a little fun with this. It's not like I want to make a good impression for my date. That was a lost cause from the moment Antoine picked me up.

"Baby, it doesn't mean anything, I swear." Then I make a snap decision to go big or go home. I press my body into Marco's side, reaching up and cupping his jaw, earning his fiery gaze. "I thought I'd spice things up a bit. I thought you'd like this game . . ." I purr, loud enough for Antoine to hear.

"What the fuck?" Antoine mutters but I don't miss the flash of heat in Marco's eyes. *Now he's getting with the program.*

"Princess," he rumbles. "You gotta let me know when you want to spice things up a notch." He wraps an arm around my waist, his large hand claiming my ass. We may be pretending but there's nothing fake about the shudder that travels throughout my body. The flash of heat I catch in his eyes tells me he didn't miss it, and better still—he likes it.

"Oh I'm so not into this shit," Antoine says, getting to his feet. "Tell Hayley thanks for nothing."

Marco and I both watch him pull out his wallet, slam some bills down on the table, and stalk across the restaurant and out the front door.

"Oh my lord, that was awesome," the waitress exclaims, giving us a small clap. Suddenly, I feel all the eyes in the room firmly fixed on us and the scene we just made. Marco looks down at me, lips twitching. "You're one of a kind, princess."

I tilt my head. "And right now, you're my favorite knight in shining armor."

My body stills when I realize I'm still pressed tightly against him, and he's still holding me close, and neither one of us seems to be in a rush to change that situation. But unfortunately, we can't stand like this forever so I gently shift back and mourn the loss of his body heat against mine as I put some distance between us.

"So . . ." I say.

"So . . ." he replies, his lips turning up into a grin. "We can either stay here and eat whatever on earth he ordered for you?

I dip my chin and look at what could just be the most pretentious, beautiful—but *not* something I would have ordered--appetizer I've ever seen—and it's not my cup of tea. I look back to Marco. "Or?"

"*Or* you can come back with me to meet my family, then I'll take you out and feed you."

"Oh my God," I gasp. "I ruined your family dinner! I'm so sorry!"

His eyes crinkle. "Two things," he says, closing the distance between us. "One, I'm the birthday boy and my family knows I was coming over to save you." My lips part. "And two, Mama wants to meet 'my realtor,' who seems to have stolen part of my brain."

My brows jump at that. "I've stolen your brain?"

"Part of it."

"Which part?" I ask coyly, unable to wipe the grin from my face.

He dips his head, bringing his face close to mine. "That's yet to be determined. But let's not keep Mama waiting."

He bends down, grabs my purse, and straightens. Then he laces his fingers in mine. "By the way, princess. Anytime you wanna play games like that, count me in."

I gasp. "I don't . . . I wasn't . . ."

He turns and grabs the bottle of red wine off the table, then winks at me. On anyone else, it would be jerky, but on Marco . . . *damn*.

A minute later, Marco and I are standing in front of a table full of Rossis all smiling up at us.

Marco might have saved me, but with all the expectant eyes now looking at me, I think I've just jumped out of the frypan and into the fire.

Luckily, I have a fireman by my side to save me.

6

MARCO

"Everyone, this is Renee. She seems to have lost her dinner date, so I've invited her to join us."

My brothers all stand and hold out their arms to shake Renee's hand, as does my father, except the sly dog looks at me and kisses her knuckles, winking when I don't stop the soft growl rumbling in my chest. Mama doesn't miss it, though; neither do Skye and Val. All three women grin at me.

I look down at Renee, who, gratifyingly, doesn't look fazed by the gauntlet I've innocuously laid down. It was purposeful. I just couldn't help myself once I saw the asshole next to her make a move. I was halfway across the restaurant when she put the asshole in his place.

Then she shocked the shit out of me. Not that I'm complaining about her pressing up against me the way she did. The ass-grab was as much for the game as it was for me, but her blown pupils and wry smile told me she wasn't complaining either. "You can let her go, Marco. I don't think she's going to run away *just* yet," Gio says with a smirk

I look back to Gio. "Maybe I don't want to let her escape?"

"The fact you're throwing her to the wolves before even taking her on a date? Big mistake, Marco. *Huge*," Skye says as the rest of my family chuckle.

"You're welcome to join us," Mama says. "Son, get your friend a chair."

I reluctantly release my grip on Renee's hand and grab a chair from an empty table beside us, dragging it next to mine. We finished dinner awhile ago, our personal chef having long finished throwing hot grilled food at us.

Once Renee is seated, I sit next to her, draping my arm behind her back

"I'm sorry for intruding. Marco just unwittingly saved me from a disastrous dinner," she says.

Papa chortles. "Renee, my dear. The way my son moved over to you? There was nothing unwitting about it."

I shake my head, glancing at the beautiful woman beside me and noting the half smirk curving her lips. Her amused gaze meets my curious one before she turns back to Papa. "Your son has made it a habit of saving me."

I dip my head as if tipping a hat. "All in a good day's work."

"I'm sorry for disturbing your meal. The birthday boy here was very insistent," she says.

Mama waves her hand dismissively. "You're more than welcome. Any friend of my children is a friend of mine." She lifts the espresso in her hand, then leans forward in her seat. The rest of my family shift back in their chairs as if they're getting ready for the show. "We're almost finished anyway. But enough about that; tell us about yourself, Renee. My son has talked about you."

I have—but I haven't said anything about how I've spent all week

*imagining those long tanned legs and those fuck-me heels I'd really
love to have in my bed.*

The princess quirks a brow my way. Her eyes are bright and
sparkling with mischief. "He has, has he?"

I shrug. I'm not going to deny it. Even if Mama *is* playing it up.

"Well, my Skye here tried to meddle, which means he kind of got
ambushed at dinner last weekend."

"I really should apologize for my sneak attack with Gilly," Skye
says,

Renee laughs quietly. "It's okay. Gilly was able to give me some
good intel on your brother so it was quid pro quo in that respect."

"Oh, I like her," Val says, nodding approvingly. "She's not going to
be a pushover."

"My Marco needs a strong woman."

While Mama, Skye, and Val talk amongst themselves about my
dating life, I lean down and bring my mouth to Renee's ear. "I'm
starting to regret not walking you straight out the door."

"And miss the free entertainment that is the Rossi family dynam-
ic?" she whispers, pulling back to meet my eyes. "My night is looking
up already."

"You know, if you'd accepted my date invitation, I would have at
least fed you before trying to feel you up."

She sighs melodramatically. "If only you'd asked."

"What if I asked now?"

Her gaze drifts down to my mouth then slowly back to meet my
eyes. "I'd say feed me and you can have anything," she whispers with
a wink. *Fuck, this woman is going to kill me.*

"*Anything?*" I ask. Her eyes flash.

Her stomach growls and she covers it with her hand, her cheeks
blushing pink as she drops her head and giggles before looking back.
"Yes, apparently, anything."

"I'll feed you if you agree to go on a date with me."

"Deal."

"Now?"

She frowns in confusion. "Now?"

God, she's cute. "Yeah, now."

"But your family . . ." she replies.

"They'll understand. We've finished anyway. And birthday rules apply."

"Birthday rules?"

"Birthday rules—whatever I want, whenever I want it, and a new one—whoever I want it with," I say with a grin

She narrows her eyes suspiciously. "That's not a thing."

"It's *my* thing."

Renee rolls her eyes and bites her lip, and now all I can think about is kissing her, tasting her, and doing *other* things too. *And yep, that's got me hard as a rock.* I can see her mind working. and I decide to choose for her.

Standing, I reach out my hand for hers. "C'mon, princess. You can get grilled by my family next time. But now, I need to feed you." When she gets up from her chair, tangling her fingers with mine, I turn to face the table, meeting a hoard of amused grins and curious gazes.

"Thank you for dinner. Renee and I have plans, and since she hasn't eaten, I'm going to see to getting her fed." I meet Mama's eyes. "I'll call by tomorrow." My mother doesn't miss what I'm not saying. *Give me this and I'll tell you what you wanna know next time.*

"Yes, son. You two go do your own thing." Mama stands and moves around the table toward us, pulling me in for a big hug, then— not surprisingly—does the same to Renee.

"It's lovely to meet you, *bella.* I hope to see you again." Then she whispers something in Renee's ear, making my date giggle then nod at Mama. *What's that about?*

I look between Gio and Luca. "I'll see you guys later."

"Run, nine a.m.," says Gio, his way of asking if I'm coming home.

"Yep. Wake me up at eight."

He nods, his lips twitching. *Right, enough of this.*

"Bye, everyone." I wave again and start moving away, bringing Renee with me.

"Bye! Nice to meet you all," she says as she follows my lead.

We walk outside and I don't stop till we're around the corner and I know we're out of view. I turn to face her, finding a wry smile twisting her lips.

"So . . ." I say, my eyes roaming her face. She's even more beautiful than I remember, and she was already stunning.

"So . . ."

"Where to?"

Her head jerks. "Oh no, Lieutenant. This is all on you. My only demand is that you feed me. Beyond that . . ."

"Beyond that, I'd feed you then work you over until you've worked up another appetite," is what I'd say if I wasn't trying to be a gentleman. That's how I know there's something different about Renee.

Do I want her in my bed? I've known that since the minute I laid eyes on her hair, her legs, those fuck-me heels I want digging into my hips, and that spark she has that's begging for me to ignite it.

But I want to get to know her. She's funny and cute and gives back as good as she gets. She's strong and independent. The way she took control of her asshole date proves that.

It's been a long time since a woman has occupied my mind like this, and even longer since a woman has met my family.

"Let's go get the princess fed then," I say, squeezing her hand. "Do you like burgers?"

"Am I Renee Hamilton? Of course I like burgers."

"Good. Then I know just the place." I take my time to slowly look down her body, pausing to take in the sexy as hell heels adorning her feet before returning to her beautiful face. "Can you walk in those shoes?"

"You've got a foot fetish."

No, I have a you *fetish.*

"I'm contemplating a fireman's hold," I say with a loaded grin.

I don't miss the hitch in her breath and make a note to go all caveman on her when we get to the point of her being naked and willing in my bed. She's not the only one who likes playing games.

"I can walk," she says huskily.

My mouth tips up in a smile. "You just let me know if you can't. I'm born to serve."

"I bet you are."

We move down the street, turn at the corner, and head down toward my favorite little diner I always come to when I'm in this part of town.

"So, why were you on that date? That guy was definitely not worthy," I ask, moving closer to her as a group of twenty-something girls walk past us.

She sighs. "You're not the only one who likes to help people."

I turn and quirk a brow.

"Hayley works for the Chicago Fire soccer team, and he's a new import that she wanted to make a good impression with."

"And your sister recruited you to do it?"

"Yeah. It was a favor—that's all."

I look her up and down. "You did *him* a favor. You made him look like he was almost worthy of having you on his arm."

She tilts her head. "Is that your way of telling me I look good?"

We stop at the lights, waiting for the pedestrian signal. I turn to face her and bring her in close, my gaze locked on hers.

"Good is nothing. You look fucking fantastic."

Her eyes soften and she blushes beautifully. "Thank you. I do try."

I lift my hand to cup her jaw and tilt her chin up. "You don't have to even try. But when you do, you'd make any man want to stalk across the room to claim you."

Her teeth dig into her bottom lip, drawing my eyes there. *Fuck, I want to kiss her.*

But I won't. Not yet. That first kiss is going to be memorable. It's going to be burnt into my brain and hers. When it happens there will be absolutely no doubt in her mind where my head is at when it comes to Renee.

"Fuck, you're cute. You're strong and tough and you take no shit, but when you're soft and pliant and biting your lip?" My voice is rough and thick. "You make me want things."

"Things?" she breathes.

"Yeah. *Things.*"

"What kind of things?" she asks curiously.

"I'll tell you when I know you won't bolt."

She opens her mouth but the lights change and we're moving again.

After that, she falls quiet and I just enjoy the feel of her hand in mine and the fact I have time with her, just the two of us. It feels right —like, *really* right. But I'm still conscious of the fact she has baggage when it comes to men in uniform—especially firefighters. I want to get us to a point where we can unpack that. Only when I know the reasons why—once we've gotten to know each other more—will I know the fight I'm up against to get her to let me in.

Which means we have to take this slow.

It's a good thing I'm a patient man when it comes to getting the things I want, and right now, I want Renee.

An hour and a half later, I'm pulling my car into her driveway and cutting the engine. I turn toward her and find her head leaning against the headrest and her soft, tired eyes looking my way.

"Food coma?"

"Close to it. You weren't kidding about those burgers. And those deep-fried pickles and ranch were to *die* for."

I chuckle. "Yeah. I go there as much as I can."

"You can take me back whenever you want."

I shoot her a warm grin. "You asking me out for another date?"

Her eyes sparkle with amusement. "If it's *those* burgers and *those* pickles, then yes. Yes, I am." A yawn escapes her, and I decide it's time to get my princess to bed. Not *my bed,* but there's no doubt in my mind that she'll be there soon enough. I'll bust my ass to make sure she does.

"Wait there," I say, hopping out and rounding the hood. I open her door and hold out my hand for hers. I'm addicted to touching her. It settles me. The warm slide of her palm against mine, the trust she gives me when she looks at me—they both point to good things on the horizon. When you face flames daily, you need something or someone to keep your mind focused on getting out. Someone to come home to and help you through the good times and the bad.

After just a few weeks and one burger date, I know Renee could be that person for me. A full heart, a good soul, a strong, resilient constitution.

And to think, we only crossed paths because Skye dragged me along to a house showing.

I lead her up the stairs to her front door. She turns to face me, the soft, gentle smile on her lips enchanting me. "Thank you for turning the night around."

"You know . . . if this was our first date, I'd be angling for a goodnight kiss."

She graces me with a slow-growing smile. "Is that what you want this to be?"

My eyes burn into hers as they roam her face and fixate on her full, glossy lips. "I know I've never had such a relaxed, easy time with a woman before tonight—date or otherwise."

She tilts her head to the side in a way I've noticed she does a lot. I get the feeling she's looking for any tell that I'm full of shit and just telling her what I think she wants to hear. "I bet you say that to all the girls."

I move in slowly, closing the distance, my gaze locked with hers. I leave barely an inch between us, the heat from her body radiating onto mine, making me ache with the need to do *something*.

"I'm saying that to the woman who's been stuck in my head for the last two weeks." I lean in, bracing my arm on the wall beside her head. My heart thuds against my chest as I breathe her in. "The woman whose path continues to cross mine. I think it means she's meant to be in my life . . . or she's a stalker."

She giggles, shaking her head and biting her lip again. I can't tear my eyes away from her.

Whatever this is between us, it's palpable. The air around us is so electric, it's like it has its own force field. It's something no one in their right mind could—or should—ignore.

I reach out and gently tuck a loose tendril of hair behind her ear, lightly brushing my fingertip over the side of her face and down the satin-smooth skin of her throat, leaving goose bumps following in my wake.

I dip my head, bringing our lips closer until they're almost touching. My eyes stare deep into her soft, glazed ones and fuck, it's a good look on her. "The same woman who was on a date tonight with a man so far beneath her, he's lucky he even got past drinks," I finish.

She lifts a brow. "And do you think you're worthy of a date with me?"

Oh, yes. There's that sass I like so much.

"Fuck no. But that doesn't mean I won't work my ass off to make sure I'm the lucky bastard who gets a shot with a show stopper like you."

She stills, her breath catching, her lips parting. "A show stopper?" she whispers, her fingertips flexing against my chest.

I press her deeper into the wall. "Yeah. The one who makes me want to buy a ticket because I know deep in my bones that if I play my cards right, she might just be the headline act for the rest of my life."

Her entire body jerks before she grabs my jaw in her hands and crushes our mouths together, her tongue delving between my lips and seeking mine. I snake my hand around her waist and down to her ass, holding her to me as I take over, kissing her deep and long and wet, not leaving a single inch of her mouth undiscovered.

She moans into my mouth and I groan back into hers, her hands roaming over my chest and waist and sliding down to my—

I end the kiss before we pass the point of no return and my aching hard-on takes this where I really wanna take it, especially after having had a taste of her.

Meeting her lust-filled eyes, I watch her lick her lips, which makes me want to take them again. I cup her jaw and trace her mouth with the pad of my thumb. "Fuck, you can kiss."

Her lips quirk up. "You're not too bad yourself, Lieutenant."

"Thanks for making my birthday wish come true."

"Thanks for letting me."

"I'm busy until Thursday, but I'd like to cook you dinner."

She melts into me. "That would be nice," she says softly. *And there's that soft spot I knew she was protecting.*

"Good," I murmur, my eyes fixated on her wet, swollen lips and I lean down to brush my mouth against hers. "You better get inside before I try and make another wish come true." My voice is so low and rough, there's no mistaking my meaning.

"What might that be?" she asks teasingly.

"That's definitely an IOU conversation."

"I might hold you to that."

I kiss her again, this time soft and slow, pulling back after touching my tongue to hers. I flatten my hands and slide them down her sides to her hips before I straighten and gently pull her off the wall.

There's no stopping my smirk at the promise of that. "I hope you do."

7

RENEE

Marco – Hey princess. What are you up to?

Renee – Hey. We're just at our grandmother's house for dinner. It's a Hamilton family tradition to watch trashy TV and eat comfort food on Sunday nights.

Marco – I like that. Let me know when I'm invited.

Renee – Whoa, buddy. Slow down. I've still gotta see whether you can bring the goods on this epic first date.

Marco – That kiss should've told you everything you needed to know

Renee – It was definitely enlightening . . .

Marco – It was something. I just wanted to see whether the DC contacted you after last night.

Renee – DC?

Marco – Douche canoe

Renee – That's a perfect name for him! But no. He hasn't texted Hayls either.

Marco – Damn. So I don't get to hunt him down and teach him a lesson in manners?"

Renee – Ha ha. I appreciate the thought but that's one battle I can probably fight on my own.

Marco – I'm sorry. I'm a little protective sometimes.

Renee – I hadn't noticed . . . but thank you for offering to give the douchebag a much-needed and overdue reality check. Somehow I think he's past being helped now.

Marco – Then let's not waste any time talking about old news, and focus on Thursday.

Renee – Let me check my diary . . . I've got an enema booked; that's the highlight of my Thursday.

Marco – WHAT?

Renee – Kidding. That's not something you'd tell the guy you wanna kiss again and who you want to kiss you again.

Marco – Oh . . . well, this is awkward then.

I gape at my phone, going back through the messages and wondering if I misread something or—

Marco – Jesus, no response. You thought I'd wanna cook you dinner on Thursday if I didn't want to see you again? Princess, I didn't think we'd need to work on your confidence. You KNOW you've got it going on.

Renee – I have some baggage. What can I say?

Marco – My mission is now to help you process that baggage and take it out with the trash.

Renee – And how do you plan on tackling that?

Marco – By reminding you every time I see you just how into you I am.

Renee – Wanna enlighten me?

Marco – Really fucking into you, princess.

Renee – Now it's awkward . . .

Marco – I'll just wear you down with my persistence and sensational cooking skills, and if those fail, I'll have to pull out the big guns.

Renee – I've always said to start with your best weapon.

Marco – I'm saving myself for marriage.

Renee – City Hall is open.

Marco – Wow. That was easy.

Renee – Ha ha. Maybe my sister's approach to her love life is rubbing off on me.

Marco – Wanna rub it off on me too?

I burst out laughing at that, earning a curious glance from Hayley who's sitting on the other couch across from me.

Marco – Shit. I didn't mean literally. I meant figuratively. As in ha ha, I'm not easy either and sometimes I swear it would be easier if I was.

Renee – Life would be easier if you were easier? You should put that on a bumper sticker.

Marco – My godson, Jake, just told me I'm an idiot who doesn't deserve a decent woman since I can't even text properly.

Renee – Well, I haven't blocked you yet, so your skills must be passable. And how old is your godson? 'Cause he sounds like a genius.

Marco – Fifteen going on forty. His father and I swear he's smarter than both of us put together.

Renee – You let fifteen-year-old boys read your texts? I'll make sure I don't send anything X-rated.

Marco – I don't usually show him my phone, so you're safe to send whatever you like…

Renee – LOL. I think I love him. Tell him to look me up in ten years if he's single.

Marco – Good to know I might have a ten-year life cycle with you.

Renee – Depends on whether you live up to expectations. You might not get past Thursday yet.

Marco – Expect the worst, princess, then I'm guaranteed to knock your socks off.

Renee – I'll hold you to that.

Marco – If you're the reward at the end, you're worth the effort.

I blink quickly to stop the threat of tears from taking hold. What the hell is this man doing to me? I'm a strong, backbone-of-steel badass who takes no shit, yet sweet words make me melt? I don't even know who I am anymore.

Renee – So Thursday?

Marco – Two options. Your place or mine, but both include me cooking you dinner. Then, if I haven't given you food poisoning, I thought we could go see the lunar eclipse at the planetarium.

Renee – Damn, Lieutenant. You're already blowing my last date out of the water.

Marco – In all fairness, that's not exactly hard.

Renee – True, but I'm looking forward to it regardless. I like the idea of you in my kitchen. Do you do dishes too? Is it a full-service dining experience?

Marco – Define full service? And of course I do the dishes. I want a date, not a maid.

Renee – If I was a swooner, I'd so be swooning right now.

Marco – I'll have to work harder then. I like the idea of you being weak at the knees and melting into me.

Renee – I was half expecting an "on your knees" joke then, but I remembered that would be a Scotty thing to do.

I snort at my joke, mainly 'cause it's true.

Marco – And now Jake and Rhodes are looking at me like I've lost my mind 'cause I'm chuckling at my phone.

My phone chimes again.

Marco – Hey, it's Jake. I just read Uncle Marco's last text and I have two words, Renee. YOU'RE WELCOME. P.S. He's never asked me for advice about women because he's rarely met any that have left an impression. He can be trained though. He has potential, I promise. So hopefully soon it'll be ME thanking YOU for making him happy.

Marco – By the way, this message will self-destruct in the ten seconds it takes for him to come from the kitchen with a beer. If he asks, I said nothing.

I leave it at that; there's no way I'm going to reply and dob Jake in it. He might be a worthwhile ally in the future, depending on whether Marco proves to be just as honest and genuine and trustworthy as he seems to be.

I'm hopeful but not fully sold yet. I've never thought a woman with half a brain should go all in from day one—or week two, whatever. As I said to Marco, that comes from my own baggage. Although the weight of it may be heavy, I'm determined not to let the hang-ups from my past dictate my future. That's why I'm giving this thing with Marco a chance, because I believe in fate, I believe in serendipity, and I believe in chemistry.

And since I was gearing up to jump on and ride that Italian stallion home last night. Chemistry is definitely not a problem for us. Not. At. All.

"Who has you grinning like a schoolgirl texting her boy crush?" Gram asks, snapping me out of my Marco daze.

"She's probably texting her new *boyfriend*," Hayley says, smirking over at me. Gram's eyes widen before sparkling with mischief, and I know I'm in for a grilling, 'Gram style.'

She turns my way in her recliner, the comedy we were watching on her TV all but forgotten now.

"So, tell me about him," she says, her lips curving up.

"A real man will never break your heart. He should break your headboard, your bed . . ." She leans forward, her sprightly eyes darting between Hayley and me. "Maybe sometimes your special place, but never your heart." She narrows her gaze my way and points a finger at me. "Is this Marco a good man? One worth your time and womanly charms?"

If anybody else said those two words, I'd bust a gut laughing, but this is Gram's way. Ever since she took us both in at ten and twelve, she has never been anything but straight to the point and honest. Then, when I moved to Chicago ten years ago, Gram came with me. Together with Hayls, we're peas in a pod—except Gram has always wanted her own space in case she ever found a man to measure up to our grandpa who passed away just before we moved.

"He's . . . he's different," I say thoughtfully.

Gram lifts a brow. "Explain, sweet child, because different could mean a lot of things, good and bad."

"The pull between us is intense, and he keeps saving me."

"You're not a woman who needs to be saved."

"No. But he's always around when I need him to be."

Her lips form an o, whereas Hayley just grins and nods. "I knew there was something strong there at the club. I could feel it."

I snort. "Surprised you could feel anything with the number of champagnes you had under your belt."

My sister's eyes narrow. "Hey. Ladies' night means fun night. Am I right, Grams?"

Gram just shakes her head, a little smile playing on her lips. "I do remember having a lot of fun when champagne was involved. Once, Hattie, Kendra, Bette, and I had a girls' night in and we shared a few bottles, and by the time my sweet George came home, he found us having half-naked piggyback races in the backyard."

I cover my mouth, but Hayley and I dissolve into a fit of giggles.

"What did Grandpa say?" I ask.

Gram shrugs. "My George knew what he was getting into when he married me. I'm not sure anything we did ever shocked him. He'd just smirk and shake his head, and then make sure I made it up to him later," she says with a wink.

I groan and Hayley just laughs harder. Gram has always been unashamedly honest with us girls. Her version of the birds and the bees talk was one for the ages and went into graphic detail that left us half-traumatized yet strangely grateful later in life. When it came to our bodies, boys, and sex, there were never any surprises.

"Is he better than the last one?" Grams asks.

"*Sooo* much better," Hayley says with an enthusiastic nod. "And hotter."

I groan and drop my head back against the sofa.

"Renee?" Gram asks. "What's wrong?"

I turn to meet her eyes. "He's a firefighter," I say softly. "And we know how that turned out last time."

Gram covers my hand with hers. "Is he anything like that ass wipe?"

My lips tip up in a smile. If anyone was to hate my ex more than I do, it'd be Gram.

"So far, so good," I say with a shrug. "He's coming over to cook me dinner on Thursday."

Gram's head jerks. "He's cooking for you? Damn, child, lock that man up and hide the key. My George was good at a lot of things—making food was not one of them. And you know what they say about men who can cook . . ."

"What?" I ask curiously.

Her eyes light with mischief. "They're good with their hands." When she waggles her eyebrows, I lose it completely, and all three of us laugh.

On the drive home, Marco sends me one last text for the night.

Marco – Sweet dreams, princess. Looking forward to Thursday.

And try as I might, I can't wipe the smile off my face or pop the small bubble of excitement inside me. Maybe Marco is everything he seems to be: strong, kind, funny, reliable, honest . . . Maybe it's time for me to stop overthinking things, because if that first kiss was anything to go by, I'd be a fool not to give the man a chance, his profession be damned.

8

MARCO

I dish up the chicken parmigiana with steamed broccoli and green beans and, after folding the kitchen towel over my shoulder, I carry them out into Renee's dining room.

Her eyes come to me as soon as I walk through the door, her gaze warming as I slide the plate in front of her.

"*Buon appetito*," I say, nodding to the food.

"Damn. He cooks, he speaks Italian. . . your talent knows no bounds."

I grin at that. "Don't get your hopes up. I know maybe ten words and I'm a so-so cook."

She narrows her gaze and I try to keep a straight face, but my twitching lips mean I fail miserably. She knocks my leg with hers. "You're so full of shit. This smells amazing."

"Have to pull out the big guns if I want another date."

Renee lifts her glass of white wine to her lips, her brow arching. "Already planning another date?"

I reach out and gently lift her free hand to brush my lips against her skin, my eyes locked with hers. "Gotta lock you in early before I lose my shot."

"You haven't done anything to minimize your chances so far."

My grin widens. "Good to know."

"Except maybe delay me eating this amazing-smelling food."

I reluctantly release her hand and hold my drink up between us. "To *official* first dates and gorgeous company." A blush colors her cheeks as she gently clinks her glass against mine.

"To men who cook and swoop in to save damsels in distress," she replies.

I chuckle and shake my head. "Something tells me you're not a person who needs saving often. You're one of the most headstrong, determined women I've met, and I'm related to three half-Italian women who would kick my ass without any hesitation if I ever put a step wrong."

Her beautiful eyes soften, a wry smile playing on her lips as she lowers her glass and picks up her cutlery.

Instead of doing the same, I watch as she cuts off a small piece of chicken and takes her first bite. Her eyes close and she hums a satisfied moan that has me needing to adjust myself. Everything about this woman intrigues me. In some ways, she wears her emotions on her sleeve; in others, she's a locked treasure chest I'm aching to crack open.

"How did you learn to cook? Your mother, or for self-preservation as a single man?" she asks.

"A lot of column A, a bit of column B. But I've only ever wanted to be a firefighter so that doesn't work if I don't look after myself. Can't pass the annual physical and do the Tough Mudder if I'm eating takeout all the time."

Her head jerks back. "The Tough Mudder? That's the dirty obstacle course, right?"

"Dirty obstacle course sounds so filthy coming from your lips," I say, my eyes drifting down to her mouth.

Renee's eyes dance with mischief as she quirks a brow. "Everything I want to say is probably not appropriate for a first date."

I lean forward in my seat. "Say it, just once. Just for me," I whisper, looking from side to side conspiratorially.

She laughs, her whole face lighting up. "So are you part of a team or . . .?"

"Our whole crew is doing it against another firehouse in six months, and all the money we raise goes to the winner's chosen charity."

Her whole face softens. "Who's your charity?"

"Big Brothers Big Sisters."

Renee's eyes light up and she smiles over at me. "I go to their charity ball every year. I used to volunteer when I was at college."

I look at her in wonder. "How are you single?"

Her lips tug up on the side. "I could ask you the same question."

"I've already told you."

"You did?"

My smile broadens. "Yep. I was waiting for my show stopper."

"Ah yes," she says, watching me over her glass. "I do remember that."

"So, you?"

"Waiting for a knight in turnout pants?"

I throw my head back and laugh. "I know you're no fire bunny. Your sister said you don't like firefighters."

She shrugs but I don't miss the blink-and-you'd-miss-it fall in her expression before she quickly catches it. I decide to backtrack and get back to safer territory. She'll tell me in her own time. It's up to me to show her I'm not the same as her ex—whoever he is and whatever he did. Do I have my suspicions about the kind of man he might've been? Sure. But I also know what people say about making assumptions.

"Okay. Tell me about your family. Is your grandmother your only other family in Chicago?" I ask, after a few moments of comfortable silence as we start eating.

"How did you remember that?"

"Remember your grandmother? You said you were at her house the other night when I was with Rhodes and Jake."

Her lips twitch.

"And I know he texted you when I left the room," I say with a chuckle. "That boy is the best almost-man I know."

"I'm thinking he's got good male role models in his life then."

"He and Rhodes lost Lily five years ago. I went through the academy with Rhodes so I've been around for all of Jake's life, but when Lils died, the entire firehouse rallied around them. The two of them might as well have the last name Rossi—they *would* if Mama had her way."

"That's amazing. Jake's already proved to me he's an impressive young man. And smart. I figured he deleted all evidence of his messages to me."

"He did. He just made sure to screw with me after doing it so I had no idea what he said but he told me he'd appreciate gratitude when he's in his twenties."

She smiles. I want to make her look like that over and over again. *Huh. How about that?*

Renee rests her hand around the stem of her glass. "So, my gram . . ." She tilts her head and looks at me. "She's the best, most nimble eighty-year-old woman I've ever known, and she was there for us when nobody else was." She pauses and stares into my eyes. "Did we want heavy on a first date?"

"If it was an *official,* official first date, then maybe we'd stay on the surface, but I want to get to know more about you—*all* about you— which means we can go as fast or slow as you feel ready to go. The rest can be like an onion."

"Layer by layer?" she says softly.

"Absolutely. Because I don't think I'll ever get tired of delving deeper and discovering all that makes up you."

She shakes her head. "You're one of a kind, Lieutenant."

"And we haven't even slept together yet," I say jokingly.

"Things you say aren't what I'm used to hearing from the men I date."

"*Or* you've been dating the wrong men, because any man who just wants a quick lay shouldn't be wasting a woman's time with false promises of more. Or, worse still, leading her on thinking it's going somewhere when he's not in the mindset to entertain anything past convenient sex on tap."

She stares at me, her breath catching, her fork stopped in mid-air. Quickly recovering, she takes the mouthful then studious eyes watch me, so much going on behind them as she takes another sip of wine.

"Usually, hearing a man say these things—things a woman like me wants to hear—would make me roll my eyes and scoff and write them off as just some guy trying to get into my pants."

I put my hand up, my devilish smirk unrelenting. "I'm gonna put it out there that I'm absolutely, one hundred percent not opposed to any part of me getting into your pants. Hell, it doesn't even have to be in. I'd be happy with *on*."

When Renee responds with an arched brow and I can see she's trying hard to keep a straight face, I wink and she cracks up, her infectious giggle making me laugh with her.

"Okay. So let's stay away from heavy for tonight. I promise I'm not hiding anything. I just like talking with you and eating this delicious food," she says. "If you were aiming to impress, you've succeeded."

"I wanted to dazzle."

"You've dazzled me."

"Wait until we see the eclipse. That'll *wow* you."

"I'm looking forward to it," she says, her grin as gratifying as it is satisfying.

I nod to her half-eaten plate as I reach over for the bottle and top up her glass. "Then eat up so we can get this date on the road. Unfortunately, a lunar eclipse waits for no one."

She gasps dramatically. "Not even the great Sir Marco Rossi?"

I chuckle. "Not even for me. Now, eat."

She gives me a mock salute. "Yes, Lieutenant."

I shake my head as I return my attention to my own plate "Smartass," I mutter.

If I wanted a meek woman, I wouldn't have been drawn to someone like Renee. And judging by how this date is going right now, I'm so fucking glad I was.

———

I stand beside Renee amongst the large crowd gathered on the big grass clearing next to the Adler Planetarium.

In front of us, there's a giant projector screen that's been set up for those who want a magnified look at the full moon lunar eclipse, which is almost due to start.

Even standing here now, I still haven't let go of her hand, loving the physical connection. I've always been a demonstrative guy in relationships—not that there have been any long-term or even serious 'I could spend my life with this woman' ones. Many haven't been happy with my hours or the danger aspect of my job, or supportive enough to accept my dedication to furthering my career. So when I started getting a little older and looking to make headway in my personal life, I became a lot more selective on my dating choices. This meant fewer options because my focus was on quality over quantity, and two of the most important parts of that are honesty and equality.

"It's starting," Renee says, squeezing my hand. I don't miss the shiver in her voice. It may be late summer but it's also a crystal-clear night, and there's a chilly breeze coming off the lake which has brought the temperature down to the high fifties.

I shrug off my jacket and hold it out for her, helping her slip it on and zip it closed.

She turns and puts her hands on my shoulders. I look down and wrap my arms around her back, lowering my head and brushing my lips against hers. Her fingers glide up into my hair and hold me there, her tongue sneaking out and teasing mine before retreating. Accepting her invitation, I tighten my hold and press her harder against me as I deepen the kiss, loving the way she meets me stroke for languid stroke.

"Thank you," she whispers against my lips when we pull apart, our eyes locked together, and I love the sexy-as-hell lust I see shining back at me. I know she can see the same reflecting back at her because I'm not hiding a single feeling when it comes to this woman—or the incessant hard-on I seem to have whenever she touches me. It would be a problem if I didn't want her to feel exactly what she does to me.

"You're kicking ass at this first official date gig," she says, smiling up at me. She turns her head slightly, burying her nose in the collar of the jacket and inhaling deeply. "It also helps that your cologne smells really good."

The announcer's voice fills the air. "The lunar eclipse is due to begin in the next few minutes. It will be visible to the naked eye— thanks to the weather gods for tonight's clear sky—or you can watch the magnified view from our telescope on-screen." With the show about to start, I frame Renee's hips with my hands and spin her slowly toward the screen again, wrapping my arms around her and pressing a barely there kiss to the back of her neck. When she covers my hands with hers and leans against me, I know I've read her right.

That's how we stay as we tip our heads up to the sky and watch the amazing sight of the sun's shadow being cast onto the moon.

Once we get back to Renee's house, again, I find myself standing on her doorstep, looking into the same eyes I was on my birthday five nights earlier.

This time, I didn't save her from a date; I was busy showing her what a date *should* be like.

And, judging by the look she's giving me right now as she leans back against her front door, I think I got a passing grade.

"Do you want to come inside?" she asks, her eyes hooded.

Fuck. Do I ever.

I move in, my eyes not leaving hers for a second—not until our hips meet and I let my gaze drift slowly down as her tongue darts out to slowly wet her parted lips. *Fuck me.*

I touch my forehead to hers. Our bodies are pressed tight from chest to thigh and everywhere in between. I huff out a breath and a frustrated growl escapes me. "You have no idea how much I want to say yes."

Her lips quirk up as she runs her hand around to my back and slowly glides it lower until she reaches the top of my ass. "Can you be persuaded?" she asks roughly.

I roll my hips against her. "What do you think?"

She laughs quietly, her fingers giving my butt a gentle squeeze. "So why can't you stay?"

"Because I have work at seven, and I don't stay out on school nights."

I lift my head back as she tips her chin and shoots me an adorable playful pout as Renee moves her hands around to smooth her palms up my chest.

"That is a real shame, Lieutenant," she says, shaking her head slowly, her eyes warm and understanding yet still full of heat.

I quirk a brow. "Rain check?"

"Oh," she says. Her smirk proves the amusement I hear in her tone. "Is this a little case of payback?"

"Believe me when I say I have far more creative and satisfying ways of dishing out payback that would make the both of us sleep well tonight—if there was sleep to be had." Her body trembles against me, and it's gratifying as hell.

"But," I say, before leaning in and brushing my lips achingly slowly against hers. "I want you to keep my jacket until next time."

She pulls back and scrunches her nose up. "Next time?"

"How about next Saturday? Wear it to my house when you come to cook dinner for me."

Her eyes flash before they grow hooded and amused. "*Oh*, really?"

"Yeah? Are you asking or telling?"

"Telling," I reply without missing a beat.

She hooks her hands around the back of my neck, bringing my face close to hers. "And why's that?"

"Because," I rasp, my voice thick with lust. I touch our lips together. "If you cook, I'll take you to bed after and have *you* for dessert."

"Damn, you're good at this," she breathes.

"Princess, you give me this rain check and I'll prove just how true that is at the first opportunity we get on Saturday night."

Renee flexes her fingers and traces the tip of her tongue along my bottom lip before I growl into her mouth and put all of my sexual frustration into a deep, wet, hard and *long* kiss, which ends with our tongues tangling together and Renee's calf hooked behind my thigh.

My hips grind against hers as I press her into the door and make out with her like the horny teenager she's turned me into.

"Saturday," I whisper.

"You're on, Lieutenant," she replies, smiling against my lips. "But you bet my ass I'm doing the dishes this time."

9

RENEE

Fridays have always been my favorite day of the week. Aside from the obvious introduction to the weekend, it is also the conclusion of another week of working hard towards a better future.

Today is especially good because after a private showing of my still-not-sold deceased estate property—the very one that brought Marco into my life—an offer was presented, and following some pretty minor negotiation, I'm now in the office boardroom with my real estate broker/boss, John, and a very happy young family of four, ready to sign on the dotted line.

As with all of my other sales, I haven't told anyone about this one because I'm superstitious when it comes to counting my chickens. It's probably why I took my time warming to a certain lieutenant too.

With all the formalities taken care of, I stand and shake their hands, laughing when the wife pulls me in for a hug and whispers, "Thank you," in my ear.

I walk them out, handing them the bottle of champagne I bought to commemorate their new home with, and wave them off as they disappear down the road.

Returning to the boardroom, I find John sitting back in a chair, hands on his head, manspreading like he was born that way. His eyes and smile are pinned my way. "Another one in the books, Ren. What does that make it now?" John asks.

I grin at him as I gather together all the sales paperwork from the table. "That was lucky number one hundred and fifty in Chicago."

"Congrats. We should all go out to celebrate," he says, looking up at me.

John is a nice, respectable, decent man—he's just never done it for me. I'm a woman who knows pretty early on whether there's potential for anything past friendship. John is a good friend, an awesome broker to have at my back, and reliable to a fault. What he's not is a ten years younger Italian American who makes my heart race at the mere thought of him, who turns me into a klutz whenever I'm near, and who has me sleeping next to his jacket just because it *smells* like him.

He's also not the first person I'd want to call about good news, like a milestone house sale. A certain Chicago firefighter, however . . .

With the signed contract papers in hand, I straighten and focus my eyes gently on John. "I'm actually having a quiet night in because I've got big plans tomorrow night." Big *plans.* Huge, *if what I've felt of Marco so far is accurate.*

"Oh. Well, good for you," he says, standing and walking around the table. "Then I won't keep you any longer. Make sure you get some downtime this weekend. You've earned that much at least."

"Thanks, John. I'm planning on it." *Sometimes down, sometimes top, and then maybe standing up if Marco has enough stamina.*

God, what is with me? Ever since Marco's dirty promise of dinner and sex, the latter part of that sentence has been the only thing I can think about. I'm not a virgin—far from it—and I'm not a prude, but it's not healthy to spend an entire week thinking about the sex more than the dinner before it, or seeing Marco's house for the first time, or even just the man himself again. I almost feel guilty about it but then I realize it's Marco's fault for kissing me breathless, pushing me up against my house—something which he seems to like doing—and putting all these dirty thoughts into my head.

"Good. You deserve it. I forgot to ask—has there been much interest in the Gold Coast apartment and the duplex the owners are selling as well?" John asks, referring to Gilly and Ezra's two listings as he leans against the table

"I've given a list of some of my existing clients to Elaine to call; we've had some bites on the marketing ads. Now it's just a case of doing the showings we've got planned and then hoping we get offers."

John nods. "That's what I like to hear." He glances down at my black patent leather pumps. "You'll have ten more pairs of those in no time."

My love of heels is not a secret around here. My female coworkers make it a point to ask me about my shoe-buying exploits whenever they see me.

"And to help you in that, I might have a few very interested buyers for you. I'll email you their details and you can follow up if you want to."

"Absolutely. That sounds great. Thanks so much, John."

"It's my pleasure. Now, hand me that contract and get out of here. Go start your quiet night in early and I'll see you Monday." He claps me on the shoulder and walks out of the room.

I check the time and see it's just after three o'clock. Marco is working but he's also said to message him whenever I want. The other night he had some downtime while on-shift and we were texting back and forth for a good twenty minutes before they got a call-out and he had to go. With this in mind, I pull out my phone.

Renee – Hey, Lieutenant. I have good news and the first person I thought to tell was a certain brown-haired, coffee-eyed firefighter I know. Is he around?

A few minutes pass before the three little dots appear on the screen.

Marco – He just left. Will I be an adequate stand-in?

My lips curve up.

Renee – Maybe. Do you have any jackets I can borrow? I seem to have a new habit of acquiring that particular item of men's clothing.

Marco – Sorry, I'm all out. I left mine with a sexy realtor to guarantee she'd see me again.

Renee – That's very sneaky.

Marco – It is, but I made my intentions for our next date very clear so I'm hoping she'll return the jacket tomorrow.

Renee – And if she turns up without said jacket because it's now got a new home in her room where she can smell it whenever she wants?

I can see he's typing his reply but he keeps starting then stopping again. I'm moving toward the boardroom door when my phone starts vibrating in my hand.

"Hey, Lieutenant. This is unexpected."

The sound of him chuckling in my ear sends a wave of warmth through me. "I couldn't work out what to say without it sounding dirty so I figured I'd go to my office and call you instead."

"It's nice to hear your voice."

"You too, princess. How's your day going?"

"I could be cheesy and say it's so much better now that I'm talking to you, but that would be one of your lines."

"Still nice to hear it though. It means I was on your mind."

"When are you not these days?" I murmur, half to myself and—obviously—to him

"If it helps, that affection is entirely mutual and not at all unwelcome on my part. I'm looking forward to tomorrow night," he says, his voice dropping to that low and melts-warm-chocolate tone I like. *He so knows the effect it has on me too.*

"So . . ." I say, trying to redirect the conversation before it gets too deep. I'll do deep, just not when the man in question is on-duty until seven a.m. tomorrow morning.

When the phone goes quiet for a little too long, Marco's soft chuckle breaks the silence. "Princess, are we running out of conversation topics already? You said you had good news . . ."

That makes me smile. "No. I mean, yes."

"Which is it, beautiful?" I can hear his amusement.

I frown. "You distracted me with your sweet-talking."

"You're the one giving me thoughts I can't entertain at work, *Ms.* Hamilton."

"I'll *try* to behave. Especially if you don't like it . . ."

"You can give me all the dirty thoughts in the world. Wherever. Whenever. I'll deal. Especially if you're the one responsible."

"And why's that?" I ask coyly.

"Because then it means I'll have a stockpile of ideas to play out in person when you're laid out naked in my bed."

"Damn. Now you're giving *me* inappropriate ideas while *I'm* at work."

"Seems like we're torturing each other then."

"Why's that?"

"Because we both have to wait twenty-four hours until we can act on any of these thoughts."

"Well . . ." I say, leaving him hanging.

"Well what, princess?"

"I can act on some of mine. It's just, you'll only be there watching in my imagination."

"*Fuuuuuuck,*" he curses, making me smile. "You don't play fair."

"What if I promised not to act out anything until we're within touching distance?"

"That would only make it *slightly* better."

"I'll take it into consideration."

His low chuckle in my ear sends a shot of heat straight through me. "You do that. Or else I'll make you tell me in graphic detail *while* giving me a blow-by-blow re-enactment."

"Blow-by-blow?"

"If I play my cards right, fuck yeah."

I huff out a breath, fanning myself as I do it. "It's lucky I'm good at multitasking then, Lieutenant."

"If you weren't, I'm a really good instructor."

"Oh, you *are*, are you?"

"Mm-hmm."

The phone falls quiet except for the sound of his breathing.

"You said you had good news?" he asks, confusingly.

"I did? Oh wait, I *did*. You distracted me with all your non-dirty, dirty talk."

"Non-dirty, dirty talk? You sure know how to wound a man's ego."

"I didn't mean . . . What I meant was—"

"Princess?"

"Yeah."

"I'm just messing with you."

I sigh, resigned to the fact that for all Marco's pros—and so far, there are a lot—his only con is his love of winding me up. "I'm getting used to that."

"Aww, baby, if I promise to kiss it better will that make it up to you?"

My lips quirk up. "Depends what you're kissing."

His responding groan is music to my ears, and I'm the one snickering this time.

"So, yes. Good news. I sold the house we first met each other at."

"That's great. Congratulations." His voice is full of warmth and pride. "We should celebrate."

My breath catches. "What?" I whisper, my throat getting tight.

"You had a win; we should celebrate. Renee, what's wrong?"

"Nothing it's just . . . I didn't even tell you that it's my one hundred and fiftieth sale in Chicago."

"Even more reason to celebrate, but now, we need to go big. I was going to let you off cooking tomorrow and whip something up myself, but instead, let's go to Wrigley for the Cubs' night game."

"*What?*"

"That is, if you want to, I mean. I'm not exactly going to let you cook your celebration meal. My mama would never let me live that down if she found out."

I open my mouth to say something but I'm still in shock.

"Do you not want to go to the game? We don't have to." The sound of fingers hitting computer keys fills the line.

"There are seats on the second level near the visitors' dugout, but I promise I'll buy you a Cubs shirt so no one mistakes you for a Brewers fan."

That snaps me out of it and my forgotten sass returns. "I am *not* a Brewers fan."

"Oh I know, princess. You seem a little shell-shocked so I had to pull out the big guns to snap you out of it."

I narrow my eyes even though he can't see me. "I'm seriously starting to think you get off on annoying me."

"No. But I do like riling you up, because then you give me that smart mouth and *that* gives me a reason to shut you up."

"You don't need a reason. Feel free to shut me up whenever you like," I retort.

He chuckles. "Good to know. I'll remember that."

"Are you seriously booking tickets right now for tomorrow night's game?"

"Nope."

"No?"

"Already booked. Just paid for them. You can still bring my jacket though—that deal *definitely* hasn't changed. And pack an overnight bag. You're staying the night."

"Sleeping in your bed?"

"In my bed? Yes. Sleeping? Probably not."

And with that, Marco has proven that yes, it *is* possible to have a spontaneous mini-orgasm from words alone.

"Marco . . .?"

"Yeah, princess?"

"You're really good at this."

"That's funny. I was just thinking the same about you."

"I'm going to go now because otherwise, I'll start telling you about my inappropriate ideas again," I say, my voice soft and husky.

"You can thank me by showing me all the best ones tomorrow after the game."

"Now *that* I can do."

"I think I'm looking forward to that more than the game now," he says, just as the bells start ringing in the background. He groans in my ear. "Sorry, baby. I've gotta go."

"I know, Marco. I know what that sound means."

"And that's something else we'll be talking about tomorrow, along with why you're so surprised whenever anyone wants to do something nice for you. Until then, drive safe and have a good night, princess."

"Look after yourself, too."

"Always, but especially when I have a night of no sleeping planned with a certain pretty lady coming up. I'll text you tomorrow. Bye," he says, before ending the call, leaving me sitting in the empty boardroom with a goofy grin on my face, my stomach full of butterflies for the first time in a long time.

Baseball and a sleepover with a man I can't stop thinking about. I don't even care that he wants to talk about my past. I can't expect Marco to be completely open and honest with me if I'm not willing to be the same with him.

So far, everything Marco has done has me wanting to see where this might go. He's the first man since my ex who's had me feeling that way.

In other words, it's about *damn* time.

10

MARCO

"For it's one, two, three strikes, you're out . . ." we shout, singing loudly with the rest of the crowd in the seventh-inning stretch.

Our seats are amazing. I lucked out with the location—one level up and directly behind the Brewers' dugout. Of course, the Cubs are up, but this rivalry is one for the ages.

Renee is as into the game as I am. She cheers when there's a hit, and groans when there's a strikeout.

We've eaten ballpark hotdogs and refillable pop. We've had a beer or two as well, and so far, it's the best date I've ever had. Papa always used to joke that if you find a woman who understands baseball, you lock her down. Watching Renee with her new blue Cubs jersey, her favorite first baseman's name on the back, I can imagine more games, more dates, more *everything* with her.

"Wanna make a bet?" I ask, nudging her with my elbow.

She turns suspicious eyes to me, her lips tipped up in a smile. "What kind of bet?"

I lean in so she's all I can see—even though that's been the case all night so far anyway. "A dirty bet," I whisper.

Her gaze drifts down to my mouth then slowly back up again, making my jeans tighten. "Bring it on."

"If your beloved first baseman strikes out, *I* get to decide what we do the second I get you alone and behind closed doors."

Her eyes flash with heat as she arches her brow. "And if he gets a hit?"

"If he gets a hit . . ." I murmur, moving my mouth to her ear. "You get free rein in my bed." She bites her lip and there's no mistaking the flash of heat in her gaze.

"Anything?"

I grin, loving the way she's leaning into me. "*Everything*. . .then again I don't really care if he gets a hit, cause even losing means I still win anyway."

I straighten and rake my eyes over her, loving how expressive she is and how she's not hiding a single reaction from me.

Her lips curl up into a salacious smile. "Okay then, Mr. Rossi. No bet, but my man will hit on the first ball. Guarantee it!"

Her expression goes from smug to hot as hell, her pupils blown, her cheeks flushed and her front teeth biting into her bottom lip. *Fuck the game. I want her now.*

She tilts her head and smooths her hand slowly over my jean-clad thigh. "Let's just see who comes out on top then."

My cock pulses at the promise in her eyes. Two and a half innings and a thirty-minute train ride until we're alone. I'm sure I can make it . . . well, I fucking hope I do.

I may want to rush home but when I get Renee all to myself, we'll be taking things slow. I'm going to take my time. Because when you've got a show stopper in your bed, you damn well make sure she wants to stay there.

———

"Hey," Renee says as I open her door and hold out my hand. We caught the train to downtown from Wrigley Field and then I drove us the rest of the way back in my truck.

But the entire trip home I've been tense with anticipation. This isn't just a random once-and-done hook up. *She* isn't someone I've just met and who I don't have plans to see again. This is the start of something. And I can't screw this up.

She hops down and I shut the door behind her, then turn to her and all but pull her toward my front porch.

Renee tugs on my arm to stop me. "Marco?" Her gentle giggle snaps my focus, and I spin back to face her.

"Yeah, princess?" Closing the distance between us, she presses her body against me and lifts up on her toes, cupping my face in her hands. With her eyes locked on mine, she places a barely there kiss on my lips. I grab hold of her hips to keep her in place and tilt my head, an invitation she does not miss. This time the kiss is slow, starting soft then turning harder, stronger, deeper. My flimsy hold on restraint snaps as my hand slips around to her gorgeous ass, my other sliding up between her shoulder blades, holding her body hostage as my tongue plunders her mouth. Groans and moans from both of us fill the air.

We pull apart, leaning our foreheads together. My chest heaves as I suck in a much-needed breath, trying to cool my jets just a little so that this night isn't over before the real fun starts.

She glides one of her hands behind my neck, her grip gentle but firm. "You're a total stress magnet, and as cute as it is to see you a little ruffled, I was worried you were having second thoughts. We don't have to do anything you don't want—"

I slam my mouth down on hers again, not wanting her to misconstrue my nerves as second thoughts. This time, though, I'm not standing by and just kissing her.

Without breaking our lips apart, I lift her up by the ass. Her legs wrap around me straight away as I kiss and walk, carrying her up to the porch. I gently lean her back against the side of my house while I find the house key, turn it in the lock, and make quick work of opening the door.

I walk us both through it and shut it again with a swift backwards kick of my foot. Renee buries her face in my neck as I carry her up the flight of stairs and down the small hallway to my bedroom. All the while her nails bite into my back through my shirt, the slight sting making me hard as a rock and even more desperate to get this woman naked.

I close my door, kissing Renee with renewed hunger. My heart threatens to beat right out of my chest as her grip on my shoulders tightens and I slowly lower her down to the ground so she stands right in front of me again.

Her half-open eyes are full of heat, her lips swollen and puffy, and I can't help the satisfied growl rumbling in my throat knowing I'm the one turning her on like that.

Then it's like something snaps and we're all over each other like animals. We're hands and fingers and lips and mouths, only pulling apart to tear my T-shirt over my head and for me to utter promises to buy her another Cubs jersey as buttons scatter across the room when I grab hers and jerk it off her. Then we're kicking off our socks and sneakers and her hands are at my belt, snapping it out of my pants, slapping the buckle against my skin and making me grunt. That still doesn't stop us. I kiss away Renee's giggles and turn them into moans as I flick open her jeans and jerk them down her legs, not stopping until she's gloriously naked before me.

Then I slowly step back and drag my hungry eyes down her body and back up again, my fist wrapping around my straining shaft out of instinct. I pull my hand back and forth at the very sight of her.

"Fuck, you're beautiful," I murmur, my voice rough and deep and laced with need.

She tips her chin, studying me the same way as I did. Her eyes unapologetically rake over my body, stopping at particular parts of interest and showing absolutely no shame in doing so. Her lips tip up in a half smirk as she moves closer, lifting one hand to cup my cheek and dropping the other to cover mine on my cock. Then she pulls my head down, touching her mouth to mine at the same time she takes over the long slow strokes along my cock from base to tip.

She traces the seam of my lips with her tongue, making me growl and driving me right to the limit of my self-control. Then I snap, attacking her mouth with renewed hunger, swallowing her whimpers, and relishing in her moans. Her body trembles against mine and her hand speeds up. My breaths come hard and fast when her grip tightens around my shaft.

I cradle her close and put a knee in the bed, gently lowering her down onto the mattress. Lying on my side next to her, I tangle my fingers in her hair and hold her in place before plundering her mouth.

I glide my hand down her body, watching her closely when I rub the heel of my palm against her clit. Her eyelids flutter closed and her head presses into the pillow as my fingers toy between her legs, a rough moan escaping her lips. My hips rock against her, my cock desperate for friction of any kind. I watch her face as I slowly inch a finger inside her slick heat, her body sucking me in, wanting to keep me there. *There's no other place I want to be.*

Renee grabs my face and crushes her lips to mine, my head spinning at the intoxicating lust I'm feeling and how crazy she's making me feel.

Tearing my mouth from hers, I pepper her neck with open-mouthed kisses, nipping gently, then soothing the sting away with a swirl of my tongue as I taste every inch of her sweet, smooth skin. I drag my lips down between her breasts, cupping them in my hands, loving the weight of them against my palm before taking one pert nipple into my mouth.

I alternate between sucking soft then harder, studying her body as her moans get louder, her grip on my hair tightening when I draw out one finger from inside her and push in two.

Her back arches. Her husky whimper fills my ears, her hips thrusting into my hand as if begging for more. My mouth waters as I lick and nip my way down her stomach until my shoulders are between her thighs, keeping her open to me. I glance up her body and lock eyes with hers as I take a long, languid lick along the full length of her wet seam before burying my face and pumping my fingers in and out of her pussy, my tongue circling and sucking and twitching against her clit. My hand grips her waist and fights her bucking hips as she rolls up against my mouth, unintelligible words spilling from her mouth in between her cries and whimpers and low, breathy moans.

Her legs hook over my shoulders and her feet digging into my back, holding me hostage—if a willing servant could ever be held— and her entire body tenses tight like a coiled spring. I slowly push a third finger inside of her just as I wrap my lips around her clit and lightly scrape my teeth over the swollen bud and she screams. "Marco. Shit. Fuck. Oh, *God.*"

She clings to me, continuing to cry out my name as her body convulses with her climax. I ease back and slow it down, my tongue languidly swirling and rolling around to draw out her orgasm. I'm more desperate than ever to bury myself deep inside this woman.

Rising up and over her, I cover her body with mine, her thighs staying wide as I nestle my throbbing hard-on against her.

I kiss her hard and fast again, my tongue exploring her mouth with a hunger born from weeks of wanting her to be exactly where she is now—fed by days of anticipation and fantasies of exactly how she'll feel when I sink my cock inside of her for that first time.

I slowly pull my head back and look straight in her lust-filled gaze. "I've gotta get a condom, baby, then I'm going to give us both what we want."

She arches her hips against mine, making my cock glide along her wet seam.

She arches her neck, running her tongue against my lips from corner to corner. "Hurry, Marco."

The fact she's using my name instead of her typical 'lieutenant' isn't lost on me. It spurs me on to hurry up. So I do, leaning over and jerking open my nightstand drawer and blindly rummaging around until I find purchase and pull out a gold foil packet.

Sitting back on my heels, I make quick work of the condom, rolling it from tip to base, my eyes catching Renee spreading wide for me, her hand slipping between her legs right where I'm about to be.

Renee bends at the waist and reaches out for me, pulling me back down over her. Her eyes search mine, roaming my face with a soft sincerity. The enormity of the moment cuts through my fervent lust-fueled haze. I pause to look at the woman beneath me who takes my breath away without even trying.

She holds her palm to my cheek and stares deep into my eyes. "I need you to make me a promise, Marco Rossi," she whispers.

"Anything, princess."

"This means something. I know that. But I also need you to not let me lose myself in you."

My heart is pounding in my chest, all I see is absolute honesty in Renee's eyes. She needs this. Whatever has happened in her past had her scared to give herself to someone again, but now she's here, showing me that soft, vulnerable side of her that makes me want to build a wall around the two of us and slay dragons and monsters for her.

I'll protect this woman with everything I am and everything I have, and now, she's asking me to protect her from herself. *That* is a whole new level of trust I've never been given the privilege of having before and it strikes right to the core of me.

Touching my forehead to hers, I lock eyes with hers so she gets just how much I mean the words as I press my lips to her mouth. "I'll never let you because I'm falling for the woman you are now and I don't ever want that to change," I say. I draw my hips back, crushing my mouth down on hers and burying myself deep inside my woman. And that's where I plan on staying for a good long while.

11

RENEE

I slowly open my eyes, reaching my arms up above my head and groaning as I stretch my spent and well-used muscles. I'm in Marco's bed after a night of very little sleep and a lot of orgasms—his and mine. I should be exhausted after managing only a few hours rest but my entire body, mind, and soul feel alive.

Speaking of that man . . . I roll over to find his big bed surprisingly empty. I pat my hand on top of the sheet, finding it lukewarm, which means he can't be far.

Closing my eyes again, I hug my pillow and decide to doze until Marco returns.

I wake again when the mattress shifts beside me. Looking up, I meet his warm chocolate gaze, watching as he reaches out to brush away the hair from my face.

"God, you look good in my bed in the morning."

I tilt my head with a sassy smile. "I think I could look good in your bed at any time of the day."

"I like your way of thinking, princess. Are you hungry?"

Pushing myself up to lean against the headboard, I catch sight of a brightly-colored serving tray placed on the nightstand beside the bed, a carafe of orange juice, and two plates with toasted bagels and cream cheese next to them.

"Wow. You give good sex *and* breakfast in bed the next morning. I approve," I say, not missing his amused grin.

He shakes his head before hooking his hand around the back of my neck and softly tugging me forward so our lips meet halfway. It's a gentle, probing, lazy kiss that I feel right down to my toes and everywhere in between. When he pulls back to end it, I'm already so addicted to his touch that I try to chase his mouth for another one. His cheeky grin is so cute—well, as cute as a big buff Italian stallion firefighter can be.

"You're far too good at that, Lieutenant," I say. "Breakfast and turning me on before I've even had coffee. You're just kicking goals everywhere today, aren't you?"

"As long as I score with you, I'll be happy."

I snicker and shake my head, unable to stop myself from grinning too.

"Hang on," I look over at the tray, my smile falling. "Hang on. There's no coffee. I'm sorry," I say, making moves to get out of bed. "That's a deal-breaker for m—"

Quick as a flash, I'm spun around and am flat on my back, an amused Marco looming over me, his body holding me in place from hips to feet. *Damn, he's good.*

I look up at him with an arched brow and shake my head. "You think you've found the man you want to date, and then he falls down at the last hurdle. And so close to the finish line too."

"You already came first last night," he says, his interest in repeating that feat making its case rather incessantly known through his pajama pants right against my core.

"I think . . . I might have forgotten all about that. Maybe I need a reminder. You know . . . just to ensure I'm making an *informed* decision . . ."

Marco shoots me a devilish grin before he plants a hard and fast kiss on my lips and moving off me, laughing when I groan in disappointment.

"First I feed you, then we talk, *then* we shower."

Now, I'm liking this plan. Except . . . "Talk?"

"Yeah, princess. Talk. You say things. I say more things. We clear the air and make sure we're on the same page of this story we're writing."

"Okay . . ." I say, narrowing my eyes at him.

"Hey, it's nothing to be suspicious about. I'm just the kind of guy that says it like it is, and I made it clear last night that this connection between us meant something. And since I didn't want to interrupt our post-date activities then, I figure now, before we recommence those activities, we can just chat."

"And eat?"

"Yep," he says, elongating the *P* and grinning at me as he takes a big bite of a bagel.

I gasp and reach over him, nabbing my own pastry and sitting straight. "Hey. Didn't your mama teach you about ladies first?"

He chuckles. "My mother taught me everything I ever needed to know about how to treat a woman. My papa showed me how to do it."

My heart melts. This man has so much love for his family, and I can see just how profound their impact on him has been. He's a good man. A trustworthy man. Someone who wore me down and charmed me, who's always right where I need him

How did I ever think I could resist him?

I sit to his side, crossing my legs and facing him, grateful that I stole a tee and boxers from Marco before we went to sleep. "Okay, let's talk. What would you like to know?"

Marco's head jerks. "Really?"

"Of course. I can't expect honesty if I can't be open and honest too." I point my finger at him. "And I'll tell you now, lying is a deal-breaker. I'm not a woman with many rules but that, cheating, and disrespect are my limits."

He nods, looking impressed. "Are you real? Because I swear you're fucking perfect." He leans in for a kiss, but I stop him with a hand on his chest.

I snort at the confused look on his face. "Nuh-uh, buddy. No touching the goods until the terms surrounding the touching of the goods are agreed upon," I say. "Unless you just want to just get down and dirty and talk to me *while* you're doing it?"

"I'll agree to whatever you want if I get a kiss. You're being all sassy and demanding, and it's doing crazy things to me," he says, his voice dripping with sex. *When did I turn into this crazy wanton woman who can barely think straight around this man?*

I narrow my eyes. "Marco . . ."

He straightens and holds his hands up in surrender. I take another bite of my bagel while I wait for his reply.

"So this is where *I'm* at with this thing we've started."

"You mean sex?"

"God no," he spits out, his dark eyes pinned to mine. "I would not have brought you to my bed without knowing I want this to be more. I want to see where this relationship can go." He laces his fingers with mine on the mattress between us. "I want to *be* with you, Renee. I know you've got your misgivings about firefighters, and I hope that one day you'll tell me about it. But being a firefighter is the only thing I've ever wanted to do, and I don't see that changing anytime soon. I love my job. I've spent eighteen years dedicating most of my time to climbing up the ranks. Now that I've finally met you, I want to spend some time working on that too."

I'm speechless. Like, I have absolutely nothing sitting on the tip of my tongue. I also wanna pinch myself and make sure this is actually happening because Marco is too good to be true.

His lips curve into a smirk. "Don't tell me I've rendered my princess speechless?"

"You are so much more than I ever gave you credit for." Yep—he says this amazingly honest and raw thing and *that* is what I blurt out.

"Baby," he says softly, and that one word washes over me like a soft, fluffy blanket, surrounding me in warmth as I prepare to unload the heavy weight in my gut. It's what has been holding me back with Marco, and it's time to let it go.

"My ex-fiancé was a firefighter." I sneak a glance up at Marco, his encouraging nod all I need to continue. "We were together for four years before he proposed. I thought that was my life sorted. I figured he was financially stable, I was happy and in love, and I was starting to do well in my own career. I had my place, he had his, and it worked. He worked twenty-four on, forty-eight off, and often between doing that, the catching-up-on-sleep-and-life after his shifts, and the side jobs to make extra money, he was busy and I understood that."

"The life as a firefighter's partner is not always easy."

I give his hand a gentle squeeze and send him a wry smile. "No, but for the right man, you know the work they do for the greater good, and you cherish the time you *do* spend together."

"Fuck," he curses.

"What?"

"Just when I think I've got you figured out, you say something like that and it makes me wanna lay you down and show my appreciation."

"But we're still talking," I say, unable to wipe the grin off my face.

"Yeah, we are. And I want you to know that whatever you say next, it won't change a thing except maybe make me wanna hunt a fellow fireman down and earn myself a suspension."

My mouth drops open, my eyes staring in disbelief. "You don't even know what he did."

"I can hazard a guess."

"Yeah, well, there was a reason he was always busy, and it had nothing to do with work and everything to do with him and fire bunnies wanting to slide down his inadequate pole."

Marco's lips twitch. Soon his shoulders start shaking, and I know he's not laughing at me, but more at how ridiculous it sounds.

He lifts my hand to his mouth and smiles as he kisses my knuckles. "Baby, it's a crying shame you were willing to marry a man with an inadequate pole, but I damn well hope I'm more than enough."

I snicker, then it turns into a giggle, and by the end of it, I'm leaning against Marco's shoulder and we're both laughing.

"Would I know him? Your ex?"

"I don't know. I try not to waste my time thinking about him," I say with a shrug

"I'm sorry that happened to you because he obviously didn't deserve everything you were giving him, and he definitely didn't appreciate it." He reaches up and cradles my jaw, tilting my chin so he's staring deep into my eyes. "I swear, princess. I would never disrespect you like that. I'd never intentionally hurt you."

"Honestly, I wouldn't be right where I am now if I ever thought you would."

"Fucking show stopper. Should've known you'd be fucking fantastic when I finally found you."

"Stop being swoony," I whisper.

"I'll stop when you stop me," he challenges, knowing exactly what he's doing.

I pounce. The bagels go flying. Soon, we're making out on his bed and I somehow end up with cream cheese in my hair. Luckily for both of us, Marco has a big double shower and he knows how to be creative in it.

Marco Rossi is now my boyfriend. Hayley is going to have a field day with this one.

Now there's just one more thing we have to do . . . get Gram's approval.

But if Marco can warm my cold heart, there's absolutely no doubt in my mind he can charm my grandmother. Or maybe it'll be the other way around. I guess we'll see.

12

MARCO

Sunday afternoon and our entire crew and Gio are sitting around Rhodes' backyard, having our monthly potluck get together. Rhodes, Zach and I started it a few years ago as a way of keeping our fingers on the pulse of the group as a whole. We may spend a lot of time working together during the week, but when you trust your life in each other's hands on almost a daily basis, the friendships and camaraderie we have as a group is just as important as the trust we need to have on the job. Besides, it's also good to just let loose among friends now and then. So we rotate these BBQs at each other's houses, and all bring food and drinks, talk shit, unwind, and often, decompress.

I'm still on a high after an incredible night and half the day with Renee. I'd love to rip her ex a new one, but had he not been an asshole and screwed her over, I wouldn't have my shot now—and that's something I'm eternally grateful for. Except for the fact that someone—namely, Gio—has obviously opened his big mouth and spread the news of my new relationship around the group.

"Scotty, I'm telling you. We're *not* going to be related."

"But if you seal the deal with Renee, and Hayley returns my calls, then I could be your brother from another mother," he says sounding far too into the idea.

I lean in, my lips quirking up. "Scotty, if a woman isn't returning your calls, she's just not that into you."

He scoffs. "Yeah, right. Women love the Scottmeister."

I meet Gio's amused eyes across the table from me as he joins in on this ridiculous conversation. "Here's a tip, *Scottmeister*. Women aren't into guys who call themselves *anything*-meister."

I snort, as do Rhodes and Jake beside me.

Scotty pulls his phone out of his pocket and scrolls through his contacts. "How about I call any one of these hot chicks in here? They'll all vouch for just how much they liked it."

Jake screws his face up and holds his hand in the air. "This conversation just went above my classifications rating."

"Says the kid discussing the pros and cons of free and paid porn with me just last night," Rhodes scoffs, earning a chorus of chuckles around the backyard.

"Smartass," Scotty grumbles, making us laugh harder.

"How about we change the subject and get back to talking about the lieutenant and his realtor. How are things going with the lovely Renee?" Skye asks, sitting in Cohen's lap and looking my way.

"Or not," I mumble, lifting my beer bottle to my mouth.

"Well, she *did* stay last night," Gio adds, *not* helping.

My sister lights up. "So, things are getting serious then?"

Rolling my eyes, I send pleading eyes to Rhodes to save me. He looks at me with a "What do you expect me to do?" expression. He's as private as I am about my life, the difference being Rhodes' life is all about work, Jake, and that's about it.

"Marco? You didn't answer my question," Skye says in a singsong voice that tells me she's enjoying this far too much.

"Yes, brat?"

"Is it serious?"

"It's something, and that's all you're gonna get."

She pouts. "You're no fun."

"And you're far too much fun."

"That's what he says." She leans her back against Cohen's chest, his arms wrapping around her waist.

"Hold up," Luca calls out, peering around Zach and narrowing his eyes on our sister. "*Why* are you touching her stomach?"

All eyes turn to Cohen and Skye, and his hands cradling her abdomen. He goes to move them to her hips but Skye stops him, a slow-growing grin curving her mouth.

"Brat?" Gio asks.

My gaze softens as my baby sister looks my way.

"We're having a baby!" she announces.

A round of cheers and applause fill the air. Gio gets up first, gently pulling Skye off Cohen's legs and wrapping her up in a huge hug. Luca follows, doing the same thing, and I'm stuck staring at the little brat who—try as I might—I still see as a little girl with blond pigtails and a pink ballerina dress who would always follow me around and look at me like I'd hung the moon and arranged the stars.

I'm the last to offer my congratulations, needing the time to swallow the lump in my throat. I'd never live it down if Scotty saw me choked up, even if it was for a damn good reason. I stand and make my way around to the now emotional Skye, who even with tears in her eyes and wet cheeks, still manages to pop a hip and narrow her gaze. "If you make me cry, Marco, I'll make your life a living hell," she says, absolutely no malice behind the words.

I pull her in for a big bear hug and bring my mouth to her ear. "Brat, I'm so happy for you," I murmur. "You're going to be an amazing mom." I move back but she stops me before I can step away.

"Uncle Marco has a nice ring to it," she says with a smile.

"My *favorite* Uncle Marco sounds more like it."

"That too."

"I love you, brat."

"Love you too, big brother."

"But now, we need to go deal with your husband because I don't care if you're married, we now have proof he's touched you and—"

Her eyes bug out of her head and her mouth drops open before she quickly recovers. Then she grins. "Oh, okay," she sighs, melodramatically. She's used to us three Rossi brothers riling Cohen up. Besides, he brought a lifetime of it when he broke the rule and hooked up with our sister. He's just lucky that I already knew he was a good man before he threw himself on his sword in front of us to tell Skye he loved her. "Just don't hurt the important parts. I may be pregnant, but I'm not *dead.*"

"Hey, *wife*! I heard that," Cohen says, appearing at her side and wrapping his arm over her shoulders.

Skye gazes up at him, looking happier than I've ever seen her. "You were meant to."

Cohen scowls back but with those two, it's probably just foreplay. *Eww.*

"Does this mean we *don't* get to rough Cohen up this time?" Luca calls out from where he's now manning the grill with Rhodes.

"Marco always spoils our fun," Gio moans. "Just let us get a few licks in. It'll do the boy some good."

"I'll show you, old man," Cohen says, him and Gio circling each other with their fists up like they're sparring, both with huge grins on their faces.

"You're all a bunch of teenage boys," Skye says, laughing as she sits down and leans back, watching our brother and her husband.

"Leave him alone, G," Zach says, chuckling as he brings out the

BBQ meat from inside. "As someone who *did* get punched in the face by my wife's brother, I wouldn't wish that on anyone."

"What about that time when you were too busy getting it on and you set your apartment on fire? Would you wish *that* on anyone?" Rhodes says, smirking at his new grill partner.

"Fuck," Zach replies, shaking his head. "Will I *ever* live that down?"

"No," every single one of us says in unison.

"Damn."

I move back to my chair, finding Jake with his head down, his attention on his phone.

"Hey. You good?" I ask, sitting next to him.

He looks my way and gives me a chin lift. *God, it's scary how much he's like Rhodes .* "Yeah, Uncle Marco."

I nod to the phone. "Who's that?"

"Dee Duncan. She's this big YouTube chef who's going viral at the moment. Dad watches her with me. I even catch him cheating and watching her new videos before I do."

My brows go up. "Really?"

"Yep. She likes doing traditional dishes in new and healthy ways and making it all from scratch, not out of a box."

"So no Kraft mac 'n' cheese then?" I ask, nudging his arm.

Jake's lips twitch. "I haven't had that since I was ten when you let me try and make it by myself."

"It was just lucky you had your fireman uncle nearby to limit the damage, huh?"

He rolls his eyes but I don't miss his half grin. "Whatever."

"Rhodes, Jake whatever'd me," I say, sounding like a petulant teenager.

"Jake," Rhodes calls out. "I've told you not to tease Marco with your superior intellect. You know he just can't keep up with us."

Jake sighs melodramatically. "But he makes it hard sometimes."

"I know, son," Rhodes says, nodding sympathetically. "But he seems to keep coming around so we *must* entertain him. Call it a humanitarian effort."

I chuckle, shaking my head and flipping them both off.

Jake stops the video and looks over at me with a contemplative gaze. "So, you and Renee?"

Smartass Jake has left the building—now I've got the good-man-in-training that Rhodes and I have worked hard on molding. Although, if I'm honest, he's probably the one who's had an effect on the two of us more than anything.

"Yeah," I say. "There's a me and Renee."

He smiles. "Good to hear you haven't screwed it up yet."

I bump his shoulder with mine. "Not yet. But give it time. It's still early days. We're just dating."

"You never 'just date.' You're not in or *all* in. There's no middle ground. So you're all in with her, aren't you?"

I swear, the kid is smarter than Rhodes and I combined. "Yeah. As of last night. Absolutely."

Jake must see something in my face because he screws his up. "Okay, TMI. I don't want to know anything because I may have been raised right, but that doesn't mean I want to blush when I meet Renee—which I will, by the way. I won't be able to hide the fact I know you're sleeping with her and then I'll ruin the cool points you've got going with her, and probably the ones I've got going with her too."

"She'd never embarrass you. I might, but Renee won't," I reply with a laugh.

"Just to be safe, let's just end it with 'you're dating.' You've got a girlfriend now. And we're waiting for the first screw-up so that I can counsel you on how to grovel appropriately and adequately so that she *stays* your girlfriend. Right?"

My eyes are near on bugging out of my head but even still, I find myself nodding.

"Good," he says, a satisfied grin on his face. He glances up towards Rhodes then back to me, leaning in and lowering his voice. "Now, let's talk about how we're going to get *Dad* a date because you're not such a lost cause anymore, but he's not even *trying*."

My eyes soften. "Jake. He's got to be ready for it."

"And he is. I *know* he is. But I've only got a few more years at home if I go out of state for college, and I need to know he's going to be okay and *have* someone other than the two of us before I go. So we have three years in which to—"

I snort. "Marry him off?"

"Or at least get him dating. I want to hear about him getting laid as much as I want to hear about you doing it—which is not at all—but I'd like to at least know he's *trying*. Know what I mean?"

Fuck, this kid is more fucking onto it than most people I know. He makes Scotty look like a toddler, and there's a twenty-year age gap between them.

"Yeah, Jake. You need me to help you with that goal, I'll be your wingman."

He snorts. "You probably need to be *his* wingman, not mine. I have absolutely no issues getting the ladies."

"TMI, Jake."

He rolls his eyes at me. "Whatever."

Then I decide a little payback is in order. "Rhodes, Jake's working his way through the female population of his school."

Rhodes looks our way, his eyes crinkling as he switches his gaze between us.

"Dad, Marco even said he'd be my wingman," Jake retorts, making my mouth drop open. Rhodes snickers and turns back to the grill.

I meet Jake's amused eyes and shake my head. "You're *such* a little shit."

"Yep. But you're proud as hell of me."

"Abso-fucking-lutely."

———

The following night, we've just finished up at a multi-vehicle accident where we were the first engine on scene and therefore, as the highest-ranking officer on-site, I automatically took control of the management. Just my luck, the second engine to respond was from Firehouse 22, which meant Lieutenant Nick Pierce had to cede his authority to me and follow my instructions.

Thankfully, he has a good crew; they just have an attitude problem when it comes to Firehouse 101. At least they never fail to put that aside when we're all at the same incident, and tonight was no different. But the big cloud of animosity floating above Pierce's head could not —and was not—missed by myself or any of my crew. We're just professional enough to ignore it and get on with our jobs, which tonight involved using both the K12 and the jaws of life to extract two patients trapped in two of the cars involved in the pile-up.

We've just finished clearing the scene when Nick walks up to me. I hold out my hand to him. "Lieutenant Pierce, thank you for your assistance. Engine 22 can stand down and return to base."

He looks down at my outstretched arm and then back to my face, nodding at my instruction but also twisting his lips up in disgust at me. "You can stop puffing your chest out now, Rossi. Do you know how to do that? Or do you need a demonstration on how a *real* lieutenant should conduct himself?" And there he goes, pushing my buttons needlessly.

I'm too tired and sick of his over-the-top macho bullshit to turn around and walk away like I *should*, like my Captain has *told* me to do countless times before. Instead, I just shake my head at him. "There's never going to be a time when I need a demonstration on *anything* from you, Pierce. Maybe it's *you* who needs to stand back and watch how *I* conduct myself. That's okay, though; we'll just wait until we kick your ass at the Tough Mudder." I hate that I let this guy get under my skin. I try to be the bigger, better man, but he makes it so fucking hard. Assholes see as assholes do, and this guy *really* brings out my inner asshole.

"And by all means, *Lieutenant*, if you want to flop your dick out too just to convince yourself that your *shortcomings* aren't all in your head, let's go," Luca says, taking my back.

Nick's eyes move from over my shoulder back to mine. "Oh, look. Need your brother to fight your battles for you now, Marco? My, how the mighty have fallen. The department's golden boy needs his baby bro to defend him."

"I don't need shit, Pierce, especially from you. You're the one with the problem—not me, not my brother, and not my crew. I have my entire *Firehouse* at my back but I see you don't have any behind you. Maybe it's because they find it hard to respect a man whose big head makes it hard to walk into the damn firehouse."

"You're a real piece of work. I can't wait to be there when you fall from grace. It's way past time you were brought back down to earth. You've had higher-ups kissing your ass and sucking your dick for far too long now."

"If I've had anybody kissing my ass, it's because I fucking earned it, Lieutenant," I grind out. "And to suggest otherwise is just downright insulting. Some of us don't need our dicks sucked to feel good about ourselves."

Nick's smirk widens. "Good to know you can't even get some, Rossi. I've never had issues there."

I feel Luca's anger without needing to look at him. I can also feel my squad watching from the truck, and I know they're already more than willing to wade in if I need them to.

"What you've got, Lieutenant Pierce, are issues—a lot of them. Maybe counseling could help. Maybe an ass-kicking could, too," my brother says. He's walking a fine line because he shouldn't be addressing a superior like that.

"Luca . . ." I warn, wanting to stop him before he goes too far. My brother doesn't have many faults but if he had one, it would be his temper. *Especially* when it comes to defending those he cares about.

Pierce steps forward and drops his voice for my ears only. "You've been a thorn in my ass since the academy, Rossi. I can't wait to bring you down at the Tough Mudder."

I shake my head because I honestly don't know what's crawled up his ass. Whatever it is, it's been there for fucking years. I've never seen a firefighter—a lieutenant, no less—with a god complex like Nick Pierce. It's not even that warranted. "Nick, I don't have a problem with you. My issue is with your attitude toward me as your commanding officer on-scene. I don't give a single flying *fuck* about you as a person. I didn't at the academy, when you were always coming third behind me and Rhodes, and I still don't. Now, if you're finished with this little pissing contest of yours, my crew and I are leaving, because it's been a long fucking night and I'd rather be anywhere but here."

I turn around and leave, not missing the shit-eating grins on all of the guys' faces except for Rhodes and Zach, who look concerned. Rhodes knows how much of a pain in the ass Pierce is and always has been, and the entire crew at Firehouse 22 has rubbed our firehouse the wrong way since Pierce has been there. It seems their sole goal is to beat us to each scene—and for all the wrong reasons. I'm worried that one day this unofficial 'rivalry' he has with me is going to cause a major problem. But right now, coffee and some food sound really fucking good.

What would be even better would be crawling into bed with Renee as soon as my shift ends in a few hours, but given her nine-to-five day job and my seven a.m. finish, that dream is going to have to wait until the weekend.

"Take us to the station, Luca," I say, grunting as I drop my body into the seat and close the front passenger door to the truck behind me.

"I'm sorry, Mar. I couldn't just stand by and watch him talk shit."

"I know. But he has every right to report you. You've got to watch yourself."

"Wouldn't ever trust that guy as far as I could throw him."

"Makes two of us, but he's a good firefighter. He's just got a me-sized chip on his shoulder."

"Then maybe it's *you* that should watch yourself."

"Always do, brother. Always do. Now, who's up for some food? 'Cause after that job, I've worked up an appetite."

"Hear, hear," the guys in the back answer.

I shoot Luca a smile as he starts the truck and we leave the scene in our rearview mirror. "You heard them, Firefighter Rossi. Your choice of takeout but I suggest you choose wisely because you're paying."

"What?"

With a smirk, I turn and lift a brow. "Are you questioning your lieutenant?"

"Are you acting as my lieutenant right now?"

"You bet your ass I am, especially if it means free food. What do you guys think?" I look over my shoulder and meet Rhodes's amused gaze.

"Aye, aye, Lieutenant," Luca grumbles, making me laugh. And just like that, Nick Pierce and his asshole complex are left behind and forgotten.

13

RENEE

Sunday afternoon and Marco and I are lying down on his thankfully wide sofa, watching the Cubs play the White Sox. Last night, I finally got around to cooking dinner for Marco. He still wouldn't let me do dishes, but that's okay because I made sure I rewarded him well after *he* cleaned up anyway. Then he repaid the favor, which led to us *both* needing to clean up. It was *fabulous*.

I had to pop out for a quick private showing at Ezra and Gilly's Gold Coast apartment earlier but the minute I came back, Marco claimed me, and we've been on the sofa ever since.

Typically, Hayley and I would've gone to this cross-town derby to experience it firsthand, but today is a little different, because in a few hours, I'm taking Marco to meet Grams.

And if we had gone to the game, Marco couldn't have used every ad break and mid-innings interval to cop a feel and turn me on. The only good thing is knowing he's suffering the torture of delayed gratification right along with me since his hips are wedged between the couch at his back and my ass at the front.

What's been an added challenge is staying quiet, since Gio worked a night shift and is sleeping just one room away.

Seeing that the sports channel has cut to a quick news bulletin, I turn around to face my erotic torturer, meeting his glazed, hooded eyes and pressing my front into his.

"You're distracting, you know?" I ask, my voice rough.

He quirks a brow, his lips twitching as he does. "I don't hear you complaining. In fact," he says, dipping his chin and rubbing his rough, stubbled cheek against mine, "the way you've been squirming and moaning under your breath, I think you like the fact I'm drawing this out."

"You think?" I breathe as he gently sucks my earlobe between his lips.

"If it helps," he rasps, moving his body down the couch and dragging his mouth over my neck, nipping and sucking and kissing as he goes. I bite my lip, my whimpers muffled in my throat when his hands join the party and start roaming, one drifting down my back, one cupping a breast, his thumb and forefinger rolling over my pert nipple through my thin top.

He stops and looks over my shoulder, his hands shifting from my boobs to my waist.

"Hey, G," Marco rumbles, making my entire body tense.

"Hey. Afternoon, Renee. Nice to see you again."

I bury my face in the crook of Marco's neck, a snort escaping my lips before I give up and start giggling, my entire body shaking with it.

"Hi, Gio," I murmur.

"Good shift?" Marco asks, still holding me in place, probably more for his benefit than mine since his body is *far* more obvious about its current state than mine is.

Then again. Maybe I should have some fun with this.

Since my hand is now wedged between us, I wiggle my fingertips, brushing them against his hard-on.

"Yeah. Typical Friday night. Attended a scene with Firehouse 22. He's on one hell of an ego trip at the moment, isn't he?" Gio says, walking past the couch and through to the kitchen, leaving us out of view.

"Yep. He'll learn."

"If he doesn't, I know a fair few cops that are more than willing to teach him anyway," Gio says.

While Gio is talking, I wrap my hand around Marco's cock and give it a firm squeeze. He grunts and taps my ass in warning. "Be good," he growls low and quiet in my ear.

I tilt my face so it's buried in his neck. "I always am," I whisper before running my tongue up the column of his throat.

"Got much planned today?" Gio calls out.

"Going to Renee's grandmother's house for afternoon tea," Marco replies.

"Wow. Meeting the nonna. That's a big deal." Amusement is obvious in Gio's voice.

"Grams is a sweetheart. Fierce but sweet, and one of the scariest, craziest, most overprotective women I've ever met," I say proudly, then I return to the task at *hand,* giving one last, teasing squeeze of Marco's hard length.

"Fuck . . ." he whispers roughly.

I kiss the hinge of his jaw. "Shh, Lieutenant. We have an audience remember," I whisper, then roll back over to face the TV and watch the game.

"You'll keep," he rasps roughly in my ear.

"Anyway," Gio says, walking past us and stopping at the hallway door, a steaming mug of what smells like coffee in his hand, "I'm heading out to run some errands, then catch up with Val to fix something at the spa."

"God, she needs to find herself a man," Marco mutters.

"Why does she need one when she's got three brothers to help her out? Anyway, I'm jumping in the shower so I'll leave you guys to it." His amused eyes go from me to Marco. He waggles his brows. "Just don't mess up the couch," he says, making me giggle and Marco chuckle. Gio winks before turning and disappearing down the hallway.

Now that we're alone again, Marco's hands resume their languid roaming, and he peppers the back of my neck and collarbone with soft, wet, openmouthed kisses.

"You're a menace," he rasps. "Teasing me when I can't do anything about it."

I turn my head, my amused gaze locking with his. "If the Cubs win, you can do whatever you want to me before we go to Grams'," I murmur against his mouth.

His eyes drift to the screen then back to mine, his lips curving up into what can only be described as a devilish 'I'm gonna get me some' grin. "You're on, princess."

That's when my own smile widens. "I damn well hope so. But a word of warning. Grams will know. And so will Hayley."

His head jerks back. "What?" he asks with a disbelieving laugh.

"Yep. Grams has a sixth sense about these things."

"A sixth sense about sex?"

I giggle, pressing my ass back against his still *very* interested groin. "A way of knowing when her granddaughters are happy."

Marco nuzzles the back of my neck and tightens his arms around me, holding me close. "Glad I'm making you happy, baby."

"Not as much as I am."

"Not as much as you will be in an inning's time either."

"Fly the W," I cheer with a giggle:

Marco's chest shakes behind me. "Never mind that. You'll be flying the O a few times before I'm finished with you."

"Then Grams will definitely know."

"Bring it on. If I can charm one Hamilton woman, I can charm them all."

––––––

"Oh wow, aren't you a big, strapping man," Grams says as soon as we walk into her den, her eyes looking Marco up and down. Hayley snickers and I bite my lip to hold back my own laugh. "Just imagine all the money I'd save with the handyman jobs you could do for me around the house." She turns to me. "Renee, I approve."

Chuckling, Marco holds out his hand and Grams covers it with hers. "It's lovely to meet you, Mrs. Hamilton," he says low and soft. *Damn, he's good.*

*"*Oh, son, please call me Grams like my girls do."

His lips twitch. "Okay."

I shake my head with a grin. "Hey, Grams. Remember me?" I ask wryly, leaning down to kiss her cheek.

"Could never forget you, my sweet child. By the way," she whispers, her eyes drifting past me to Marco's butt, "ten out of ten so far."

I snicker. "Behave, Grams."

"Never," she mouths back. "Now, take a seat and Hayley can get you refreshments."

Refreshments? I quirk a brow at my sister, who's struggling not to laugh herself.

I take Marco's hand and we sit on the sofa across from my grandmother. "Thanks, Hayls."

Hayley rolls her eyes. "I can do one better than that. I'll serve up food and drinks."

My head jerks back. "You cooked?"

"Well, I wasn't going to make Grams cook for all of us. Her doctor said she needs to take it easy."

"Hush now, child," Gram says, waving her off. "Young Marco doesn't need to hear about an aging woman's woes." She looks over at the young man in question and smiles sweetly. "I'm not an invalid just yet, but my sweet girls think I'm ready to be shipped off to the good lord upstairs. I happen to think I've got at least another twenty years left on this earth. There's still so much more mischief to get up to, don't you think?"

"You don't look a day over seventy, Grams," Marco replies smoothly. I cover my mouth to smother my giggles, my shoulders shaking with them. Grams narrows her eyes at me but I don't miss the flash of amusement on her face either.

She nods. "Such nice manners. A gentleman should always compliment a lady. Your parents raised you well. My George had a way with words too."

"Mama always said manners will get you far."

"She's right," Grams replies, smiling up at Hayley as she returns with a tray of sandwiches and pastries, and disappears again. Not long after, she comes back with another tray, which Marco stands and helps her with, this one with a teapot of what will undoubtedly be Gram's favorite English Breakfast tea, along with a jug of iced tea with matching tumblers.

Like the trained hostess Grams taught her to be, Hayley serves everyone, before joining Grams opposite us.

"You have a lovely home. My parents live not far from here," Marco says, looking around the living room. Grams has always prided herself on keeping a clean and tidy house. She has a cleaner come by twice a week but she still would've made sure the place was perfect before we arrived today, purely for Marco's benefit.

"Thank you. My George always loved coming home to a nice tidy house with a good home-cooked meal after his long, hard day at work.

I'm sure my granddaughters will be just as thoughtful when they *finally* settle down too."

Hayley snorts but covers it quickly with a cough, her dancing eyes widening as she looks over at me, my expression mirroring hers.

To his credit, Marco doesn't miss a beat, but he does reach out and rest his arm over the back of the sofa behind me. "I can already tell you've done a fine job with both of them, too."

I blink in shock as Gram's cheeks turn pink. Oh, my. Marco Rossi has just charmed my hard-to-please grandmother in the space of twenty minutes. My ex tried—and failed miserably—to make a good impression on her. Grams has always supported the decisions Hayley and I have made in our lives, but when it came to my engagement, I knew she was worried.

Listening to Marco, Hayley, and Grams talk, I'm amazed—but not all that surprised—that Marco has just slotted into our close-knit family of three.

"Now, Marco. You may or may not know, but we haven't had much luck with firefighters in this family," Grams says, snapping me out of my revelry. My mouth gapes open.

"Grams!" Hayley and I gasp in unison.

She arches a brow. "What, sweet child? Am I lying?"

"No, but I—"

"But nothing, Renee. Any man worthy of my granddaughter's time and body must be able to rise above the woman's past dalliances." To his credit, Marco doesn't even flinch.

"I agree with that sentiment, Grams," he replies, locking eyes with her intense gaze. He laces his fingers with mine and squeezes me affectionately. "And I can unequivocally promise you that I am absolutely nothing like that particular poor excuse for a man."

She tilts her head as if studying him, looking for any sign of uncertainty. When she seemingly finds none, she smiles at him. "I'm glad to hear that. Let me warn you—my Renee here is hell on wheels when cornered and she's as a stubborn as I am when it comes to standing her ground, regardless of whether she's right or wrong."

Marco chuckles. "Good to know."

"And she loves thoughtful gestures. Not expensive ones. She's determined and feisty and bull-headed, but she's ambitious, and when she sets her mind on getting something or going somewhere, she never gives up till she makes it happen. She loves fiercely. She's also the most loyal, thoughtful and supportive wom—"

Hayley giggles. "Grams, you sound like you're selling him on a prized cow, not your granddaughter."

"Oh pfft," she says, waving my sister off. "One look at those two and I already know Marco appreciates what he's got in his arms and his bed."

Marco's amused grunt almost sets me off. I did warn him Grams would know, and there's a dazzling twinkle in her wise old eyes confirming she's not blind and is definitely still as sharp as a tack.

"I know all about you macho firefighters." A sly smile plays on Gram's lips as she leans toward Marco, her eyes bright. "When I was a young sprightly thing, my girls and I were known to get up to a little mischief."

"Something tells me you and your friends got into more than your fair share of trouble, Grams," Marco says, making even me swoon, and I'm the one who just two hours ago was panting and whimpering under his touch as a result of a lost bet. But I clearly came out on top thanks to his talented mouth, fingers, body . . .

Grams holds up her fingers. "Maybe," she says, a sly smile playing on her lips. "But what's the point in living life to the full if you don't have fun while doing it?"

"There's fun, then there's getting stuck up a tree in a miniskirt at three a.m. on your fiftieth birthday, Grams," I say with a giggle.

Grams laughs. "Hey. A woman only turns fifty once, and in the end, I was saved by five very hunky firemen with a big ladder."

"And Grandpa blew his stack when you conned the firemen into dropping you home and turning their lights on, giving him one hell of a fright."

"Your grandfather was a good man who hooked his star to a wild woman. He knew what he was getting into, believe you me," she says.

"I think your husband and I would have had a lot in common then," Marco says before turning my way. His intense gaze and quirked lips make my stomach flip, my heart sigh, and my lady parts clench. "At least the part about having a soft spot for a wild woman."

Holy spontaneous orgasm, Batman.

"Oh, my sweet child," Grams says. "I approve. I wholeheartedly approve."

And all I see in her expression is relief, something I've never seen before. She's not just saying it, she means it, and it's not until now that I realize I really needed Grams' okay. I needed to know I wasn't just seeing everything I wanted to see in Marco. He's the real deal. He's everything he says he is, and if Grams can see it, and Hayley can too— well, she liked him before she even met him—then I can trust my gut when it comes to my growing feelings for this man.

It was never anything about Marco; it was me and my own baggage that were the problems. But not anymore. When it comes to Marco Rossi, I'm all in. With my moment of self-realization passed, I lean into his side. His hand comes down to rest around my shoulders, pulling me in closer as I melt against him. And when I sneak a look at Grams and Hayley, both of them are grinning over at us and I don't even mind.

That's until Grams opens her mouth again. "So Marco. Now that Renee's taken care of, have you got any handsome single friends for my Hayley, here?"

14

MARCO

I'm sitting at my desk, working through a pile of paperwork while the guys run through drills in the garage, when my phone vibrates against the desk.

Renee – Hey. How's your day going? I'm just sitting down to dinner with Hayley and thought I'd see how you are. Can I call you tonight? I've got something to ask you?

"Who's that?" Luca asks, walking into my office and slumping down on the small couch opposite my desk.

"Hello to you too."

"Hey, brother. How have you been in the fifteen minutes since I saw you last?" he asks.

I turn to face him, shaking my head at his shit-eating grin. "Smartass."

"One of us has to be. You'd rather moon over your *girlfriend* than do paperwork. Jeez, you get the approval of the nonna and you're all lovey-dovey and shit. I should probably check it when you're done just in case you've written 'Marco hearts Renee' or something."

I snicker, shaking my head at the idiot. "Like you've finished yours."

"Well, no. But I'm taking a well-earned break before getting back into it."

"You say that like you've even started."

"Hey, I was hungry and you can't stay looking this good without sustenance."

I chuckle because I've never met anyone else who can eat his weight in food and *not* have to slog his guts out to work it off. Luca seems to eat without regret and have it all turn into muscle, and that includes a few of Mama's home-cooked meals each week. He doesn't live there, but I swear, he'd eat there every night if he could.

"How is Renee?" he asks, nodding to the phone.

"Did I say I was messaging her?"

"You didn't have to," he replies without missing a beat.

"She's good."

"So things are going well?"

"What do you think?" I reply in a 'duh' tone.

"You're an Italian Captain America. Everyone loves you, so of course you've got the Hamilton women eating out of your hand."

"Who does that make you then?" I lift a brow his way.

"The Hulk."

I throw my head back and burst out laughing.

Rhodes appears in my doorway, looking between us with a smirk. "Is Luca telling you about how he had a woman's roommate ask to join in last night?"

My eyes bug out at my brother. "What?"

He winces and scowls at Rhodes. "Thanks, big mouth. Last time I tell *you* anything in confidence."

The grin on Rhodes face gets bigger. "Gio thinks it's funny too. The Captain and Zach just chuckled and walked away, muttering about how you'll never learn, and I think Scotty wants to ask you for tips since *Hayley* broke his heart."

"Hayley didn't even get close to his heart. All she wanted was a good time," Luca says. "That's more than half obvious."

I hold my hands up when both of them turn to me as if I know the answer. "I have not and *will* not ask Renee's sister why she hasn't returned Scotty's fifty calls and text messages."

"Fifty? Shit," Rhodes says in disbelief. "We need to teach him how to be cool."

My eyes widen. "Do you think he's going to change? He's been the same way as long as we've known him."

Rhodes sighs. "This is true."

Back to my brother, the manwhore. "How on earth did the proposed three-way come about?"

Luca blushes a little. "She told me she had a roommate and that they might be keen to join us. I was the idiot who assumed she was another girl."

I bite my lip, trying so hard not to laugh, but I make the mistake of glancing at Rhodes and we both crack up at the same time, howling this time, not having any hope of being quiet.

"God, I hate you two sometimes," Luca grumbles.

"I'm just living vicariously through you. Learning what *not* to do when I start dating again."

That grabs my attention, my head turning in slow motion to my best friend. "Did I hear that right?" I ask quietly.

Rhodes shrugs. "Jake has a point. He's gonna go to college in a few years, and I can't put my life on hold forever. Lily wouldn't want that and Jake's got a good head on his shoulders. Maybe it's time I open myself up to the possibility of *dating* again."

"Yeah. But there's no pressure." I tilt my head Luca's way. "You don't have to be like my 'easy-breezy, all access to everyone' brother over here."

"Thanks," Luca retorts dryly.

I eye him questioningly. "Am I wrong?"

"You don't have to be so obvious about it," he mutters.

"Neither do you," Rhodes says, backing me up.

"Yeah, yeah. Maybe I'll be like my big brother here and meet the one woman who knocks him on his ass and fall head over heels."

"Actually, she *did* knock me on my ass—*literally.*"

"That'll be a good story to tell the grandkids one day," Rhodes replies with a knowing glint in his eye.

God, that's jumping a bit far ahead, isn't it?

I roll my eyes and turn back to face my desk. "On that note, I need to get back to my paperwork before we get another job."

Luca stands and looks over at Rhodes, both of them with knowing glints in their eyes. "That's code for 'get out so I can call my *girl-friend,'*" Rhodes says with a smirk.

My brother snorts. "Doesn't want us to hear him getting all lovey-dovey 'cause then we'll give him shit."

Rhodes scoffs. "Says the man who only sweet talks to get in a woman's pants."

"Or skirt. Not that fussed," he says with a wink. Rhodes grabs him in a headlock and drags him from my office.

"Thanks," I call out, still chuckling to myself as I bring up Renee's number, already looking forward to hearing the sound of her voice.

"Hey," she says softly when the call connects.

"Hey yourself. You know you don't have to text me to ask if you can call? If I can answer, I always will."

"I'm not one of those needy girlfriends who expects you to reply straight away. I just like to let you know I'm thinking of you and that you can call me when you're not busy."

"Baby, if you call and I'm not on a job, I'll always answer because there's nothing better for my mood than hearing your voice if I can't see you."

She sighs, and fuck, that's a good sound. It's a happy one that tells me I'm not laying it on too thick. My doubts that we're on the same page are pretty much non-existent, but when a man has a woman in his bed he wants to stay there, he'll always be a little wary until he locks it down. "Good to know."

"What can I say? I kinda like you."

"Oooh. Like really, really like me?" she asks, putting on a teenage girl's drawl.

I chuckle. "Yeah. Like, a *lot*." I try to sound like a surfer dude but it comes out more like Beavis from *Beavis and Butthead*, making her giggle down the phone.

"That's good. It would be terribly sad to have to break Grams' heart. She's a firm fan of yours now. She's even told her friends about my 'handsome new man-friend.'"

"I promise not to break any Hamilton woman's heart."

"I'll hold you to that."

"You can hold me to anything as long as it's against your body, especially naked."

"*Behave*, Marco. Don't be sweet and sexy when I can't show you my appreciation," she says, her voice as smooth as the melted chocolate I drizzled over her skin a few nights ago when we last had a sleepover.

"Being told to behave. *That's* a first," I say with a laugh, resting my ass against my desk, my groin definitely interested in the memory and promise of more. "You said you wanted to ask me something."

"Yeah. So John asked me today if I was planning on going to the Big Brothers Big Sisters Fall Ball next month."

"You said you usually do."

"Yeah. I do. I just hadn't really thought about it."

"I can be the candy on your arm," I reply without her asking. "I think I look quite good in a suit if I do say so myself . . ."

I hear her small gasp in my ear. "I didn't, I mean . . . you don't have to—"

My lips twitch and I shake my head, even though I know she can't see me. "Renee, were you going to ask me to be your date?"

"Yeah."

"Do you want me there?"

"Yeah," she says softly and so damn sweetly that it makes me wish I was there right now to throw her over my shoulder, take her to bed and show her what she does to me.

"Then I'll be there. When is it?"

"Four weeks away. Can you make it?" she asks, and I don't miss the hope in her voice.

"Princess, I wouldn't miss it for the world. Especially since it means I get to see you in a ball gown."

She gasps. "I didn't even think about that fact. I'll get to see you in a suit."

"I'll swap shifts around if I have to, and—"

Her breath catches. "I don't want to be any hassle though . . ."

"Baby, I may not be able to give you everything in the world, but I'll never give up trying. This is important to you and because of that, it's important to me." Comfortable silence fills the line. "But also, the fire department gets tickets every year because some of us volunteer now and then. The difference this year is I'll be going for *you*, not as a firefighter. I'll get the guys to come too." The line goes quiet.

"Renee?"

"He never . . ." she says shakily but trails off. She doesn't often talk about her ex, which is good, because then I'd press to try find out who he is and likely hunt him down to thank him for being a fuck-up and giving me a chance with her. "I know you're not him, you're nothing like him, but sometimes you're so different it takes my breath away," she says in her honest way that I like a hell of a lot. There's no pretense with Renee. It's all black and white, and clear as day.

"Nothing about you will ever be a hassle. I swear to God, Renee, don't doubt how important you are to me."

"Maybe you need to come show me," she says, and I can hear the smile in her voice.

"I need to sleep tomorrow, but do you want to come over tomorrow night?"

"Or you could crawl into my bed when you finish in the morning and sleep here."

"Will you be there with me?" I ask, my voice thick.

"For a few hours, then I'll have to leave, but I like the idea of you coming home to me in the morning."

"You have no fucking idea how much I've been wanting to do that."

"Good, because I may have snuck my spare key into the front pocket of your work bag."

My lips curve up as I look out the window of my office. "For a special occasion?"

"For when you called me and I asked you to come here in the morning."

"You were rather sure I would say yes."

"I seem to know you well," she replies with a laugh.

"Fuck, princess. I swear you were made for me."

"If that's true then that means you're meant for me too."

"I'll prove it in the morning."

"I'm counting on it."

"Good night, baby."

"Good night, Lieutenant. Stay safe."

"Always do. But let me ask you something. Did you call to tell him to be safe, or is that just for me?"

"Considering I wasn't *allowed* to call him, or if I did, he'd never call back? It has only been and only will be yours. It would also be a damn shame for you to do something to yourself now after spending so much time and effort getting me to like you."

"You did put up a good fight," I say, and you could not wipe the satisfied grin off my face if you tried.

"It was a battle I had no hope of winning."

Fuck that feels good to hear. "I'm glad you didn't win. Not when we know how good it is now."

"Absolutely. Now stay *safe,* Lieutenant. I have plans for you in the morning."

"Not if I wake you first."

I smile at her soft moan. "Goodnight, princess. Don't do anything I'll have to spank you for."

"What if I send you photos?" she asks with a sexy laugh that gets my cock's attention again.

"Stop making me hard when I'm at work and can't bend you over my desk to deal with it *and* you."

"At least now I know you won't be short of ideas in the morning. Bye." She giggles before hanging up.

The bells ring five minutes later, giving me enough time to recover. Yet I still walk out to the garage with a stupid grin on my face, earning an amused chuckle from Rhodes and a shake of Luca's head. I glare at both of them. "Not a word. But we are going to the Fall Ball together, so make sure you guys are there too. We'll make a night of it as a crew."

"Sounds good to me. I'll bring Jake; he's been bugging me to go," Rhodes replies.

Luca nods. "I'm sure I can find a date. If not, Renee has a sister, right?" he asks as he sits behind the steering wheel and turns the key.

"Hey. You leave Hayley alone," Scotty calls out from the back seat. "She's mine."

I scoff and look over my shoulder. "Does *she* know that or is there a trespass order at play here?"

Scotty flips me the bird. "Maybe she lost my number," he mutters. By the time we pull out of the garage, lights and sirens blazing, the entire crew is laughing.

15

RENEE

I'm surprised to find Marco's truck still in my driveway when I get home after work. He'd crawled into my bed and woke me up in spectacular fashion before he promptly fell asleep curled behind me, while I dozed until my phone alarm vibrated on my nightstand.

He slept like the dead while I got ready. I let Hayley know he was there, had a key and would lock up when he left. I didn't expect him to be here now.

Before he crashed out, he'd told me we were going out on a date tonight, which is why I'm home an hour earlier than usual so that I'll have enough time to beautify myself to knock his socks off when he comes to pick me up. Since it seems he's already here—or rather, still is here—he'll likely distract me. I won't have the same element of surprise when he sees my outfit, but I know he'll be far from disappointed.

I put my key in the lock and walk in my front door, finding the man in question laid out on my couch, and a basketball replay on the television. He mutes the sound as I walk toward him.

"Princess, come 'ere," he rumbles, his voice rough.

"You should've just watched TV in bed. Then I could've crawled in with you, and had a repeat performance of this morning."

"Why do you think I came back before you got home?" he asks, raking his eyes up and down my body. "Now get your ass here so I can kiss you and show my appreciation for your workwear."

"What?"

"That's okay. I'll get up and come to you." He shifts as if to stand up. But I rather like the idea of lying all over him as he is.

"No," I say, "stay exactly like that."

His adorable confused look makes me laugh as I kick off my heels, drop my purse on the side table, and move his way.

"And if you like this look, just wait until you see my date outfit."

"Looking forward to it," he says with an appreciative grin just before I launch myself over the back of the couch and land flat-out on top of him with a heavy thud and a loud groan from the man himself.

I prop myself up on my hands so I'm looking down at him. "Hi again."

"Hey."

"Sleep well?"

"Yeah. I like your bed. Just like it better when you're in it with me."

"Oh yeah?" I say, my lips curving up as his gaze darkens.

"I think you should show me how much more fun it is when we're both naked and horizontal."

In the blink of an eye, I'm flipped over and we've switched places, Marco's hard muscular form pressing down against me as his lips crash down on mine.

He moves his mouth lower to pepper kisses along the sensitive skin of my neck. "You said my bed . . ." I moan although I hold him tight against me, not wanting to go anywhere.

He chuckles. "Soon."

"Okay," I breathe, and it's my last coherent word for the next thirty minutes.

———

We've just finished our three-course meal at the same Japanese restaurant where he saved me from my horrible blind date last time we were both here. On the plus side, at least I got to *taste* the food this time and choose dishes myself, too. This was after we were a teensy bit late by way of Marco having a roger rabbit moment—tongue rolling out of his mouth and all—when I walked out of my bedroom ready to leave for dinner wearing a deep cowl-necked black dress, bronzed bare legs, and my newest pair of black Fendi pointed-toe ankle boots.

"I can't believe you brought me back here," I say, lifting my glass of wine to meet Marco's raised one opposite.

His dazzling smile is almost blinding. A relaxed and happy Marco is a sight to behold. I never stood a chance at resisting this man. *God knows why I thought I ever could—or ever wanted to.*

"I wanted to give you a date re-do."

I tilt my head and frown. "But you already gave me a real first date?"

"Yeah, but when I saw you having dinner here with the douche canoe, I knew I wanted to bring you back here one day."

"You were *that* sure I'd give in to your relentless pursuit?"

He grins and shakes his head. "Was it relentless though? Or were you just ignoring all the signs the universe gave us?"

I shrug. "A bit of column A, a lot of column B."

"And now?" he asks, quirking a brow, his legs brushing against mine under the table.

"The longer we're together, the more I wonder why I was so hell-bent on resisting you."

"Because I'm too handsome and sexy for my own good?" he asks, flipping his hair back like a preening peacock and posing with his arms up, showing his bulging biceps.

"Sure, let's go with that," I murmur wryly, taking a sip of my wine. His gaze narrows, and I struggle not to giggle. Then he chuckles and I have to put my glass back on the table before I lose the fight and start snort-laughing in a dramatic fashion.

When I catch the strange amused looks from our table neighbors, I cover my mouth, my mirth turning into a soft snicker.

Marco's eyes sparkle, his attention stuck on my upturned lips. "Fuck, I wanna kiss you. I remember sitting across the restaurant from you and aching to see you smile but not wanting you to have *too* much fun with that guy, because it pissed me off."

I lean into my hand, intrigued by the insight he's giving me. "What did?"

"That you were out with him when I knew I wanted you on my arm, at my side . . ." He leans in. "And in my bed."

I lick my lips. Knowing how much he wanted me, even before I gave up fighting my attraction to him, is hot. He's certain of who he is and what he wants. He's never given up looking for his "show stopper"—and he thinks that woman is me.

That gives a woman with baggage like I have, the confidence to be herself. It's probably because when you're not looking, and a man like Marco Rossi is unapologetic in his pursuit of you, and is *sure* that you're the one he wants, there's no need for anything but the truth. I've not held back any of my faults or flaws, my likes or dislikes, or any of my personality traits—the good, the bad, and the annoying. He's been through two bouts of PMS with me and hasn't batted an eyelid or gone running for the hills. I've managed to not once doubt where he is or what he's doing when he's not working because he's done absolutely nothing to show me he's nothing but the man he's proven himself to be. I haven't been needy or demanding or anything but myself. It's been as easy as breathing since the day we first met. It's been exactly how I thought it always would be when I found the right man. *I'd just stopped looking.*

The waiter stops by and slips the check onto the table. Both Marco and I going for it at the same time, but when he pins me in place with a heated stare full of determination and the promise that he'll show his appreciation in ways I'll like later, I let him win.

His victorious grin widens, and I narrow my gaze.

"You know you're not always going to win?" I ask.

"There's no doubt, princess. You'll fight for your right to fight for as long as you live." Marco waves his arm in the air, handing the black folder with the check and his credit card to the waiter as he walks past.

"Too right," I say with a laugh.

"But here's the thing," he says, leaning forward in his seat and placing his hand over mine on the table. "I like everything about you, Renee. What I've seen, and what I haven't yet. So if you think I don't appreciate the fact you don't just sit back and *expect* me to pay the bill, then you're so fucking wrong, but you'll get there."

"Get where?"

"To the place where you stop thinking something you do could put me off or make me think anything except how fucking lucky I am to have found you."

I pinch myself to make sure I'm not dreaming. *Nope, this man is as real as it gets.*

I tangle our fingers together, giving his a gentle squeeze. "How on earth were you still single?" I blurt out.

"What?" he splutters with a laugh.

"You're hot. You're charming. You have a good job, a successful career, you treat women well, you come from a good family, and you love hard and fiercely and you do it unapologetically. You're phenomenal in bed, you give before you take—but not before giving *again*—and most importantly, you're not an asshole."

Marco's lips curve into a cocky smirk, but it just serves to make him downright irresistible. *Where the hell is the waiter? Some of us need to get out of here—like now.*

"Anyone would think you like me, princess."

My eyes widen, my hand covering my heart as I feign innocence. "Whatever would make you think that, Lieutenant?"

He barks out a laugh. "Call it an educated guess."

I hold two fingers in the air and scrunch my nose up. "Okay, I might like you a *little* bit."

Marco's eyes dance with amusement, and he's still shaking his head at me when the waiter returns with his credit card and two individually packaged mints on the small ceramic dish.

"Oooh, I'll take one of those."

Marco's eyes warm as he hands me a mint. "Planning on getting lucky tonight?"

I waggle my brows. "Play your cards right, Lieutenant, and you might find out."

He shoots me his signature 'I'm gonna get me some' grin as he pockets his wallet again and stands, holding an arm out my way.

"C'mon, beautiful. Let's get out of here."

"I thought you'd never ask."

He stops and holds the restaurant's front door open for me, pressing his palm to the exposed skin of my back, sending a delicious shiver through me.

Once we're outside, he leads us away from the main thoroughfare. Turning to face me, he slips his jacket off and drapes it over my shoulders before tilting my chin up with his knuckles and brushing his lips against mine.

"If you're up for it, I thought we could go for a walk through to Buckingham Fountain. I haven't seen the light show for a while, and we've got more than enough time tonight to do everything I've got planned for you—*twice*—and still fit this in."

"Okay," I whisper, totally breathy and obvious. "Lead the way."

Ten minutes later, we're walking hand in hand into Grant Park. "When I first moved here, I used to love coming downtown and spending the day just exploring," I say.

"Yeah? Papa used to bring us boys out to give Mama a break from all the noise."

"Probably the girls too," I muse.

"Or give us a break from them. *God*, Skye was easy compared to Val." He chuckles then turns to look at me. "She still is, too. Val takes high-maintenance to a *whole* new level."

"She seems lovely."

"She's as sweet as pie. Honestly, she'd fight to the death for anyone she cares about and would give up the shirt off her back. She's just . . ."

"Needy?"

His eyes flash. "Yep. You know something about that?" he asks, quirking a brow. I look around, trying to get my bearings in the dark, spotting the small circular fountain with the original Turtle Boy fountain figure in the center.

"Hayley is a lot of things. Not needy, per se. More . . . reliant, maybe. But she was young when we went to live with Grams so it has always just been the three of us girls—and Grandpa, of course—but just us three since he passed. And I guess she's always known we'd be there to help her out when she needs it."

"And you?" he asks, his voice soft and low.

The fountain sparks to life in front of us, the bright lights glowing against the darkness behind it. "Wow. I've never seen it at night. It's gorgeous. I used to love watching it during the opening credits to Married With Children and made sure it was one of the first things I came to see during my first visit Downtown."

I let go of his hand and turn to face him. Looping my arms over his shoulders, I tip my head and smile up at him, feeling so content, so comfortable and so sure of the person I am and the man in front of me. When he wraps his arms around my waist and pulls me in close, I melt even more. *Nothing and no one has ever felt this right.*

"You didn't answer my question, baby," he says, running a hand along my back.

I run my fingers through his hair, tugging his head down closer to mine. "I'm right where I want to be with exactly who I want to be with."

His intense stare bores into mine, and I hold my breath because the air changes between us and I don't yet know what it is. I just know it's something epic, monumental . . .

"Fuck, I love you."

I gasp but don't dare move, not wanting to do anything to ruin this perfect moment.

His gorgeous eyes soften, full of absolute certainty and sincerity. "And I know I will for a really long time, probably forever."

Tears sting my eyes because of all the things I expected him to say, that wasn't one of them. I stare at him, surprised beyond belief, but my heart feels so full it's fit to burst. I run my hands around his shoulders to cup his jaw, my thumb sweeping over his cheek as my gaze roams his beautiful face. When I lock eyes with his, I know I have his full attention.

"I love you, too," I reply. His entire body jerks then goes deathly still, my breath catching at the intensity shining back at me.

Then it's as if he snaps, his hand hooking around the back of my neck and tugging me closer. Marco kisses me hard and with so much feeling, I gasp. His tongue delves past my parted lips, circling my own as he deepens the connection, both of us giving as good as we get, cementing this monumental occasion in the only way we can in public. But I'm looking forward to continuing the celebration behind closed doors as soon as we get home.

When we finally pull apart, he buries his face in my neck.

"Fuck, princess. Just when I thought you couldn't surprise me."

I'm grinning when he straightens and looks down at me, his expression so soft and gentle it makes my heart skip a beat.

I shrug. "I was just taking a page out of your book."

He tilts his head, his brow furrowed. "And what's that?"

"When you know, you know."

"Okay then. So where do we go from here then, oh wise one?"

My lips curve as I melt into him and touch my mouth to his. "Well, I want to go home to bed so I can *show* you how I—"

That's all I get out because Marco is kissing me again, swallowing the rest of my words. Then he grabs my hand and near-on drags me back toward the parking lot.

It appears Marco isn't a fan of delayed celebrations. Which is good, because right now, neither am I.

16

MARCO

I use my key and let myself in, finding Hayley sitting on the couch, some reality singing competition playing on the TV. She looks over her shoulder and checks me up and down grinning when she meets my eyes.

"Hope you're ready, Rossi. My sister is gonna knock your socks off in a minute."

I look down at my watch and smirk. "Not sure we've got time for that, but I'm game if she is."

"Oh, eww. I mean she looks hot, you perv!" she says with a laugh, throwing a handful of popcorn at me and thankfully missing.

"Hey, you better clean that up," Renee says, walking into the kitchen and grabbing her purse from the counter. I don't move though —I can't. I'm frozen in place, taking her in from her bare neck down to the blue velvet dress that clings to her curves the same way my hands are aching to right now. Maybe Hayley was right when she said her sister would knock my socks off, because she's turned me mute and dumb with lust as well.

She turns and stares at me, stopping mid-step as her eyes rake over me with just as much hunger as I'm feeling right now.

"Hey," she says, her voice rough and sultry and *not* helping my self-control at all.

"You're killing me in that dress, princess."

Her perfectly painted red lips curve up seductively. "I really hope not, Lieutenant, because I have dirty plans for you in that suit later."

Hayley makes puking noises from the other side of the room but I'm on a mission. Regaining the ability to move, I close the distance between myself and the woman I love, lifting my hands to cradle her jaw as soon as I'm within reach.

"You look beautiful," I whisper, lowering my head.

"Wait," she says, pressing her palms to my chest. "If you kiss me how I know you're going to kiss me, I'll have to redo my lipstick and—"

I crush my lips to hers anyway, loving the way she whimpers into my mouth as I take my time. I wait till she's soft and pliant and sagging into me before pulling back and gazing down at her now swollen, smeared lips, feeling triumphant and way too fucking turned on. Especially since we won't be able to do *anything* about it until much later tonight when we're back home.

"Damn, now *I'm* gonna need a cold shower. You know it's cruel to make out in front of a single woman with no eligible men on the horizon, right?" Hayley asks. I stand beside Renee and wrap my arm around her waist, deciding not to let the chance go by to screw with Hayley just a little bit.

"You know, there's a certain single man there tonight who I know for a *fact* is going stag . . ."

Hayley narrows her eyes at me. "No. Don't you dare. That was a one-time thing. He's just not my ty—"

"Type? Really?" I ask.

Renee giggles, resting her head on my chest. "Hayls has a dream man she's striving to one day meet, and no one else will do."

I frown. "Is this an actual person?"

"No. Just an ideal. A girl has to have goals, you know," Hayley says with a shrug and a smile. "Look, I know Scotty is probably a nice guy, and maybe even a good guy—he's just not *the* guy I want to end up with, and I don't want to get involved with someone and not be available when I meet *the* guy."

"Right," I say, not understanding the logic but each to their own. I look down at Renee just as she shifts back and tips her chin to meet my eyes. "Thank fuck I'm *your* ideal guy, princess."

"You were my knight in shining armor. I had no choice."

"Too fucking right," I say, smiling against her lips as I give her one last kiss and lift my head. "Now you better go fix your lipstick because I may like the look of you messed up and knowing I did it, but I'm not sure *you* will."

She snickers and wipes my mouth with her thumb, her eyes twinkling with mischief. "That goes both ways. I'm not sure Fire Engine Red is quite your color, Lieutenant. Ironic, isn't it?"

Hayley starts up with the puking noises again, making Renee rolls her eyes. "I'll be back."

"And I'll watch you go, just so I get the *full* experience of that dress."

"You're such a perv!" she calls out as she walks down the hallway.

"You're not the first Hamilton woman to call me that tonight."

"It's 'cause we're always right."

"I'll remember that," I say, turning back to a smiling Hayley.

She nods. "It's probably best."

"You know what's also for the best?" I ask.

"Go on," she says with a resigned sigh.

"Texting Scotty to tell him you're not interested. Then maybe he'll stop telling me we could be family one day."

She winces. "Yeah. *That* I can do."

"Much appreciated."

———

Walking into the hotel where the ball is being held, I don't think I've stood taller or ever felt more invincible, and it's all because of the woman on my arm.

It's not because she looks fucking amazing—she's breathtaking, permanent hard-on inducing, the envy of all men, all of the above—and it's not because the way she carries herself exudes such confidence and an aura of success that it makes everyone want to get close, talk to her, or *be* her. It's the whole package. It's just *her.* And seeing her in her professional element tonight as she works the room, shaking hands with existing clients, potential new ones, and business contacts, I'm in awe of the woman—and I'm the lucky S.O.B. who gets to call her mine. What makes it even better is that I'm equally and completely hers too.

"Dinner will be served in ten minutes. Please make your way to your allocated tables," the event's MC announces from the middle of the stage. Renee laces her fingers with mine, and we walk over to join the rest of the guys at our table. There we find Rhodes and Jake, Scotty, Luca, Gio and Val—who all came together— and Cohen and Skye. Rounding out the group is our Captain and his daughter, London.

I introduce Renee to everyone, chuckling when she pulls Jake up into a big hug. I'm not sure I've ever seen my godson speechless before now . . . or that I've seen him blush.

"Behave yourself, midget. I'm watching you," I warn.

He quickly gets his bearings back, clutching his hand over his chest and feigning innocence. "Who, me? What on earth would I have to offer as magnificent a woman as Renee?"

Rhodes hooks an arm around his son's shoulders, shaking his head. "I'm sorry, Renee. My son here seems to think he's a bit of a ladies man."

"Says my father who has been binge-watching a certain *YouTube* chef and hiding it from me."

My best friend's mouth drops open, his eyes wide as Jake winks at Renee then turns to his dad and quirks a brow, as if challenging him to argue.

"I don't know what you're talking about," Rhodes mutters, lifting his glass to his mouth and without another word, walking around the table to join Luca and the rest of our group.

I hold my hand in the air. Jake gives me a high five and laughs, his eyes tracking his dad as he walks away.

"He so likes her," he says.

"A YouTube chef? I suppose it's a pretty safe option, since it's unlikely he's ever going to meet her," Renee replies.

Jake's eyes look between us. "That's the thing. She's from Chicago."

Renee gasps. "Oh, wow."

"How about this, bud. Let your dad do his own thing when it comes to dating and whatnot."

Jake groans and rolls his eyes. "Then he'll never do anything and he'll still be single when I move out, or I'll never leave because I don't want to leave him alone."

"You're adorable," Renee says, sidling up to the boy and wrapping her arm around his waist. "Can we keep him, Lieutenant?"

I chuckle. "How about we let Rhodes have him, and I'll let you visit whenever you'd like?"

"Oh alright then," she says, leaning in and kissing Jake's cheek, making him blush again.

I narrow my eyes but this time, nothing can wipe the shit-eating grin from Jake's face. Not even when I tell him he's got lipstick on his cheek.

"I don't care. I'm going to wear it like a badge of honor. Chicks will think I'm a catch."

"*Chicks* don't like being called *chicks*. Have I taught you nothing?" I ask, shaking my head in mock disappointment. "I'd say go to your room, but you're in public, so maybe go save your dad from Skye's pregnancy stories."

His eyes widen. "Good idea. Bye, Renee. Feel free to claim me anytime, especially when you get sick of *this guy.*" Jake nudges my arm then jumps out of reach, laughing as he moves away.

Renee smiles up at me. "He is teenager goals."

"He is pretty awesome."

She pats my chest, placating me. "Don't worry, baby. I promise not to share my lipstick with any other man tonight, okay?"

"You'll keep, princess. You'll keep." I expect a smartass reply but instead her head jerks from something over my shoulder back to me. "I just need to go to the ladies' room before we start dinner."

"I can take you if you want."

She shakes her head and brushes her lips against my cheek. "I'm a big girl, Marco. But save me a seat, okay?"

"Always."

She shoots me a smile, then turns and walks out the nearest door. I do as instructed, taking a seat next to Luca and waiting for Renee to return.

———

After dinner, the CEO of the charity finishes giving his thank-you speech, and shakes hands and takes photos with some big names holding oversized checks. I take advantage of the lull in proceedings, running my hand up Renee's thigh under the table. Ever since she returned from the restroom, she's been strangely quiet.

She covers my hand with hers and stops my advance, meeting my eyes.

"You're very distracting," Renee whispers in my ear. I turn my head and press my cheek to hers.

"Says the woman who's commando under that dress."

Her head jerks back. "I'm wearing a thong." Her gaze narrows as my lips curve into a knowing smirk.

"I look forward to discovering it later," I say, leaning close and brushing my mouth against hers. She reaches up and rubs her thumb over my lips, holding it up to show the lipstick smear she's tidied.

"Red looks so much better on you." Her eyes crinkle as she shoots me a devilish smile. "I dunno, I'm up for testing my red lipstick on other parts of your body when we get home if you are."

And now, all I can think about is *that* mental picture, and how long I have to wait to make it a reality. *Damn. My princess can play dirty.*

The MC for the event announces the dance floor is open for business. After waiting a few songs to people watch—and laugh at Luca, Scotty, Skye, and Cohen mucking around—I decide it's time.

There's no way I'm missing the chance to dance with my girlfriend for the first time and show her off as mine in front of everyone. With this in mind, I stand and hold out my arm, waggling my brows. Renee grins and places her hand in mine, standing and following as I lead her out onto the edge of the floor to a place near the crew but not too close.

As we sway from side to side to the beat, she nestles her head against my shoulder, her arms wrapping right around my back. "Thank you for being my arm candy."

I touch my lips to the top of her head. "You're welcome, princess. It's been a good night."

"Yeah . . ." The lack of enthusiasm in her voice grabs my attention.

"That sounds convincing," I reply

"It's not that."

I stop moving and she shifts back, her wary eyes staring straight into mine. I cup her cheek. "What's wrong?"

"It's nothing. I don't want to let anything or anyone ruin our night. Just forget about it."

"I *would* have if you didn't just say that." Then a light bulb goes off. I don't know why I didn't think of it sooner. "He's here, isn't he? You saw him before dinner."

She looks down, her silence saying it all.

"Hey, it's okay," I say with a gentle smile. "He's just a guy. He doesn't get to dictate what you do, where you go, or who you see now, right?"

"Yeah. I just . . . he represents the me I'm embarrassed I ever was."

"Whoever you used to be, the woman who worked the room tonight and owned it was always in there. Whoever it is, he's an asshole who didn't realize the beauty he had when he had it. He used the uniform and his job to fuel his ego. It says nothing about you and *everything* about him. Okay?"

"I love you," she whispers, her eyes shimmering with happy tears. This time, our lips meet halfway in a soft, gentle, full-of-feeling kiss that's more of a promise to each other than anything else.

"You good now?"

She tilts her head flirtatiously and beams up at me. "I'm with you. Of course I'm good."

"Aww, aren't you two cute," a familiar voice slurs behind me.

Renee's expression falls and she tenses.

"Pierce, lay off. Leave Marco and Renee to it," Rhodes says, moving closer. "We're not on duty. You can be an asshole another day. Just leave it."

I stare dumbfounded at Renee. "The asshole is Nick Pierce?" I ask incredulously.

Her fingers cling to my arms. "Just leave it, Marco. *Please.* He's not worth it." I'm angry but not at her. I didn't once suspect Nick Pierce was her ex because she never told me his name and I never asked. But the absolute last person I ever thought Renee would be *engaged* to is the thorn in my side. Mainly because I didn't think the guy had it in him to score someone as hot or as amazing as she is.

As her man *now*, and the man who plans to be by her side forever, it's my job to show Lieutenant Nick Pierce just what he lost.

I hook my hand behind her neck and pull her close, crushing my lips to hers, kissing her long, hard, and deep. It's not how I'd normally kiss in public, but needs must. Nick fucking Pierce deserves to know what he stupidly threw away. He needs to know she's mine.

I pull away and plaster a smile on my face, ignoring Renee's wide eyes and shaking head. I wrap my arm over her shoulder. Then I turn us around to come face to face with a glassy-eyed, sneering Pierce, who's looking between Renee and myself with disgust.

"I never thought you'd slum it after me, Nay, but if you're desperate enough to go for Rossi here, then you must've hit rock bottom."

My entire body stills, my muscles tensing impossibly tight and my head ready to explode right here in the middle of the dancefloor. I fist my hands at my sides, my gaze filtered red as I wait for Nick to give me a reason to justifying laying him out cold.

Renee gasps, obviously reading my body language. "Marco, he's not worth it. C'mon. Let's go home and—"

"Yeah, *Marco*. Why don't you let Renee take you home? She used to try and lead me around by my dick as well, and look how well *that* turned out."

"You did *not* just say that to me," I growl. I sense that we might've grabbed the attention of those around us now, and not just my crew either. But I'm not about to stand by and let the woman I love be spoken about so crudely, *especially* not by this lowlife.

"Was it a pity fuck?" I ask, turning to Renee.

"What?" she whispers, the word barely audible.

"This guy. Was he that desperate that he wouldn't leave you alone so you just gave in and then couldn't get rid of him? Because I've had you; you're fucking magnificent, baby, and I've also known him for years, and there's no way in hell he'd ever be worthy of you. He's not even worth the shit on the bottom of your shoe."

"Marco, *please*," she pleads, her eyes darting to the crowd. "Please don't make a scene. You're right; he's not worth it. Let's leave now. Just turn and walk away."

"Yeah, *Marco the Great.* Listen to the ball and chain. I never knew you'd be happy with my sloppy seconds. I could've introduced you two a long time ag—"

I'm stepping forward and cocking my arm before I even know it's happening. My fist flies into Pierce's jaw as Renee screams, *"No!"*

It reverberates in my ears. I don't get a chance to throw a second shot because Rhodes comes in front of me and Luca stands between him and Pierce, and it hits me like a ton of bricks what I've just done.

I spin to find Renee, but all I see is her back running out of the room and my pregnant, very angry-looking sister scowling up at me.

"Skye," I growl. I need to go after Renee. Skye stops me though, grabbing my arm and dragging me back to the table. She turns her head toward the small crowd watching us.

"Nothing to see here, people. DJ, you're up." To his credit, the man in the booth on stage does what the angry woman tells him to and turns the music up.

"Skye, I need to talk to her," I say when we reach our table. My stubborn sister just pushes me into a chair and glares at me, her finger pointed ominously in my face.

"No. You need to calm the fuck down and get some ice for your hand."

"On it," Jake says, making a beeline for the bar at the side of the room.

"And big brother, you need to give Renee some time to get home and come up with a plan to rip you a new one."

"Look. I know I shouldn't have punched him, but—"

"Oh, no. It's not even that. You're not here as a firefighter today—which is lucky for you—but it's not lucky for *her.*"

Fuck. *Fuuuuuuuck.* Skye nods, a slow, sardonic smile appearing on her face. "And *now* he gets it."

"I was defending her."

"And any other time, that would be hot to a woman. *Not* tonight. And *not* when it's clear you've got personal history with the asshole ex that represents the biggest failure of her life."

"Shit," I spit out, just as Jake reappears holding a napkin full of ice. "Here, Uncle Marco."

"Thanks, Jake," I mutter, taking it from him and pressing it to my swelling knuckles.

"Now, Cohen and I will take Renee home, and I suggest you give her tonight and start some much-needed groveling tomorrow." She's right. She's Skye, of course she's right. I was here as Renee's date and

I let Nick get under my skin and draw a reaction out of me, which is exactly what he wanted. That makes me no better than he is.

I nod, leaning in to kiss her goodbye.

"Look after her, brat." If I know Renee, she's equally parts angry and hurt right now and the knowledge that I made her feel like that is tearing me apart. If I can't make it right tonight, then at least I trust Skye and Cohen to be there in my place.

"I will, big brother," she says. "That's something I will do."

17

RENEE

I toss and turn all night and when I finally give up on sleep and get out of bed, my head is complaining about the tequila shots Hayley poured down me after I got home.

I'm still nursing my justifiable snit when Marco knocks on my door the next morning. His mouth slams shut the moment he lays eyes on me.

He walks in and takes a seat at the kitchen counter, not saying a thing while I walk past him and pour us both a coffee, but because I'm a little Petty Betty, I turn and take a slow, measured sip in front of him, not offering him his cup just yet.

"Do you want one?" I finally ask.

He nods and I move past him, leaving his on the bench for him to pull closer himself. Then I walk over to the couch and sit down in the corner, curling my legs under me.

He doesn't sit opposite me, though. He proves he's a man who likes to take his life in his hands and puts his cup on the table before sitting right beside me, leaning his shoulder into the back cushions and watching me. "I'm so fucking sorry, princess."

"Go on . . ." I say, not wanting to make it seem too easy for him. It's a given that I'll accept his apology, but he did ignore my repeated attempts to deescalate the situation, so it's only fair I let him say his piece first, right? Besides, I'd rather get all of this sorted out between us so there's absolutely nothing left to fester and grow and ruin what we have. *This is what a true adult relationship is all about—and it just goes to prove I'd never really had one until I met Marco.*

"I was an idiot, and the way I defended you? It made a bad situation worse."

"You might as well have pissed on my leg."

Marco frowns. "Nothing I did was about claiming you for his benefit."

I tilt my head and lift my brow. "Really? Because it seems to me you were peacocking like an alpha caveman just as much as he was with his dumbass drunken comments. If you'd started banging your chest and grunting 'my woman,' I probably wouldn't have been surprised."

"I wasn't staking a claim."

"Then what were you doing?" I ask, crossing my arms over my chest and pinning him with a glare. "Because if you two had flopped your dicks out to see whose was bigger, I wouldn't have been surprised."

"It's mine, right?" he asks, his lips curving into a half smirk.

"Of course it's fucking yours," I say, rolling my eyes. "But you've just proven my point."

"No," he says, his expression turning intense and commanding my attention. "Kissing you like that in front of everyone was about *me* showing *him* you're worth so much more than how he treated."

"That's not who I am now."

He squeezes my hand. "You think I don't know that? I came over this morning knowing you'd bust my balls and call me out on my behavior last night, but what we have is worth so much more than either of us ever imagined, and there's nothing I won't do to fight for that."

"Marco . . ."

"And one of the things that drew me to you is your independence and strength, just as much as your spark and your gorgeous ass in that dress you were wearing . . ."

"Hey," I say with a laugh, giving his arm a gentle shove.

"Honestly though, the woman you became *because* of that asshole is who I'm in love with. It's what makes your eyes light up and gave you the courage to fight our chemistry at every turn until I wore you down." A smirk pulls at his lips, widening when I glare at him.

"Baby, it wasn't the right time and place. I know that now, but more than anything, I wanted him to see how happy and in love you are. You're with a man who knows your worth and who will support you in everything you set your mind to. I'll always have your back, even if it means changing shifts to be your arm candy and making sure my crew makes a night of it, too—for them, for me, but mainly to support *you.* I'll always have your back the same way I know you have mine."

"Fuck, you're too good at this apology thing."

"I can't say it won't happen again, but me acting like an idiot isn't a common thing. I'll make sure those events are few and far between and when I do screw up, I'll always make it right."

I swallow down the growing lump in my throat, blinking back the happy tears threatening to escape.

"Call it pride, call it cockiness, but I wanted him to know that you're it for me like I already know you are." He leans forward and cups my jaw, rubbing his thumb over my bottom lip and looking straight at me. "There's never going to be anyone else, princess, and I know how so fucking lucky I am to be loved by you."

How the hell can I hold a grudge now? Do I have a lifetime of this to look forward to? If so, sign me up. "How can I argue with you after *that*?"

He sends me an indulgent, butter-wouldn't-melt half smile. "We could move on to the making up portion of this apology."

Seeing his hopeful expression, I shake my head and giggle. *God loves a trier.*

"You seem pretty confident there, Lieutenant. But let me say my piece first."

He nods and shifts back, but he's still close, and still touching me. It's a good thing, though; it anchors me.

"The thing is, that wasn't just a charity event for me. That was also about networking. There were a lot of past clients there and potential new ones. My biggest fear is that any ground I made earlier in the night could've been lost because we let Nick *fucking* Pierce get under our skin."

Marco grimaces. "If it helps, I know for a fact he'll get the same ass reaming from his captain as I got from mine this morning."

"Wow. That was quick."

"Cap called and made it crystal clear that Pierce and I will cross paths and will have to work together, and if we can't, then something will need to be done."

"You can't let him have that much control over you. He's not worth it. Take it from someone who learned that lesson long ago," I say, uncurling my legs and draping them over Marco's lap.

He straightens and wraps his hands around my knees. "I don't usually let him get to me. But when it comes to you, it appears all bets are off and my restraint goes flying out the window."

"Maybe find some next time . . . or, you know, listen to your girl-friend when she says it's time to leave."

"She's pretty awesome, that girlfriend of mine."

I shrug, shooting him a small, cocky grin. "I think she knows that, but it's still good to hear it anyway."

"I'll remember to make sure you always know it, princess. Look, I know I did a dumb thing, and I was too far gone to stop and listen to you. I can't say I won't screw up again in the future—'cause I *am* a man, and we are known for acting first, thinking later—but I am sorry. I was a macho dick, and I'm sorry I couldn't walk away and be the better man."

I shake my head. "You still don't get it, Marco. You *are* the better man. You don't have to even try."

"*Fuck* . . ." he breathes, his eyes searching mine for any uncertainty. "Jesus. You really mean that, don't you?"

"How can you not know that I absolutely adore you?" I say, shifting my legs to straddle his thighs. "I love you. You're the man I always hoped to find and one I least expected to fall for. But every time I'd normally start to doubt what I was feeling and how *much* I was feeling, you'd reassure me without knowing you were doing it."

"Baby . . ."

"And I get it. I didn't tell you his name so when he goaded you, you were blindsided, and you just reacted. I really didn't think I'd cross paths with him, especially not at *that* ball."

"I said the department gets given tickets every year."

"Yeah, but I've been going for ten years, and he never showed any interest when we were together."

"Ah, yes. He wasn't a lieutenant then though, was he?"

I shake my head.

"Pierce passed the exam and ever since, he's had a god complex bigger than the John Hancock building. He's determined to work his way up the ranks, whatever it takes, whatever the cost, and whoever he has to shit on to get there."

"Lovely," I muse, scrunching up my nose.

"That's *not* the word I'd use to describe him."

"Cohen mentioned something about bad blood between you and Nick but wouldn't elaborate."

"Rivalry, mutual hatred. I've just never been able to stand the asshole."

"Makes two of us then," I say, my lips quirking.

"There must've been a time you liked him enough to marry him."

"Or I was too stupid and too loyal to see the forest for the trees. I was a shadow of the woman you see today."

He reaches out and rubs his hand over my knee but doesn't say anything.

"So what made you snap last night?" I ask.

"You're joking, right? He had no right to say what he did about you. But he was looking to push my buttons and cause trouble, and that's exactly what he wanted. He just got it care of a fist to the face."

I shake my head. "So you were defending my honor?

"Fuck yeah. He's an asshole, but *what* he said about you? That was just inappropriate, rude, and completely uncalled for."

"Yeah, I get that, and I don't mean to piss you off any more, but it's not the worst I've heard from him."

"What do you mean?" he rumbles angrily.

"He wasn't a fan of me calling off the engagement," I say matter-of-factly.

"So maybe he had *some* idea of who he had and what he'd lost."

"I'm not saying he ever appreciated it; he just liked the idea of having what he thought was a perfect little wife waiting at home for him, regardless of what—or *who*—he was doing outside of the house."

"You're so much better off now."

"Without a doubt. But it's my turn to apologize because it's his baggage that made me so hesitant to give you a chance."

Marco's eyes are soft as he rubs his palms up and down my legs. "I'll let you in on a little secret."

I scrunch my nose up. "What's that?"

"Nothing is worth its weight in gold unless you have to work to get it. And you are the best thing I've ever had to fight to win."

My nose starts to tingle and my eyes sting but it's a good thing. I cannot think of a time I've been this happy.

"Now," he says, giving my hips a gentle squeeze, "before we stop talking about this, let's agree on one thing."

My lips slowly curve. "You resuming this apology in my bed?"

He smirks. "That's guaranteed. But first, nothing and no one will ever come between us. It's you and me against the world, princess, and that's how I want it to stay."

"Deal," I say without hesitation, leaning in and touching my lips to his. "Now, back to this apology of yours."

"It's a hard job, but someone's got to do it," he says with a sigh.

I wriggle my ass in his lap, earning a low, throaty growl. "Well, *something* is hard. It would be a shame not to put it to good use."

And for the rest of the morning, we both make sure it's not wasted.

18

MARCO

Monday afternoon and we're gearing up on the run as we hurry to a house-fire call, one of multiple engines responding.

Not knowing how big the fire is or how long it could take to get under control, I shoot Renee a quick text before we get too close to our destined address.

Marco – Hope you're having a good day, princess. Knowing you, you're kicking ass and taking names. Love you, always.

"Still in the dog box?" Luca asks, glancing sideways at me as I put my phone away.

"Nope. We're all good. I'm heading there in the morning."

He nods. "You guys have got a good thing. And even if you did screw up, you're one hell of an upgrade from the ex."

I don't say anything because he's not wrong.

Ten blocks away from our destination, I can already see smoke billowing up into the sky.

"It's a doozy," Scotty calls out, leaning in the gap between the front seats to get a better look.

"He's right. Game faces on, boys. It's go time as soon as we arrive," I say, just as I hear it called over the radio that Firehouse 22 is first on-scene, which means Lieutenant Pierce will be in charge until a superior officer arrives. I groan. Luca and I share a knowing look. After Saturday night, this is going to go one of two ways, and past experience with Pierce has taught me not to let my guard down—especially after what happened at the ball two nights ago. But he's in charge of running the fire, so in the end, I'll still have to follow orders.

We pull to a stop and all hop out, Rhodes and I heading over to where Nick and his second-in-command, Alex, are standing in full gear as if they're ready to head inside at a moment's notice if needed.

"Lieutenant," I say when we reach them.

Nick looks over at me and I catch a flash of annoyance crossing his features before he schools his expression and switches into professional mode. The guy may have a god complex, but he's still a good firefighter.

"Rossi. My guys are around the back getting ready to vent. I need you and your guys going in the front to check there's no one inside. Reports indicate it's abandoned, but there could be squatters like there was in that last warehouse fire, and you'd hate to have that on your conscience, right? You know, since you're such an upstanding guy and all."

There it is. Asshole Pierce is back in business.

Rhodes growls under this breath next to me, taking my back the same way I'd take his in the same situation. I put my arm out to stop Rhodes' advance. Pierce and his minion just look between us and smirk.

"Yeah, Rossi. Call your dog back and get your heads in the game. Time's a-wasting," Nick says. I can tell he's itching for a fight, but he's shit out of luck if he thinks he's getting another one from me.

"Right. We'll clear the first floor," I reply."

"Alex and I will join you as soon as a captain arrives. Ours is caught up so it'll likely be yours that takes over command."

Good. At least then I can trust standard operating procedure, or SOP, will be followed to the letter.

Without giving the asshole another word, I turn and together, Rhodes and I move quickly to the guys, relaying our orders. We all jump into action,

"Scotty, Max, you're out here watching our backs and reporting in to command until Cap gets here to take over. Rhodes and Zach, you're together, as are Luca and myself. We're all heading in to clear the first and second floor."

I don't wait for them to agree because I've always had the respect of my crew. It's why we've stuck together for so long.

As instructed, we climb the stairs and move inside, masks, helmets, SCBA and PASS devices all on, my brother next to me, Rhodes and Zach behind us. We take a side each, working our way from room to room, calling out for anyone who might be there and looking for any sign someone could be hurt, injured, or trapped inside.

We meet halfway down the hallway. "Clear at our end," I shout to the guys.

"Same here so far. Just need to check the back," Rhodes yells over the roar of the fire.

I jerk my head. "We'll start upstairs. Call out over the radio when the bottom is clear."

Rhodes and Zach nod and disappear. Luca and I move back toward the front of the house and the staircase.

A muffled message comes over the radio. The smoke is thicker now, my visibility limited to my hand in front of me and nothing more. The radio sounds again.

"Lieutenant Rossi, it's Cap here. Do you copy?"

"Yeah, Cap," I reply, tilting my head to bring my mouth to the radio clipped to my jacket.

"Luca's out. Pierce has said he'll take your back until Luca can return. Lieutenant Pierce reports the vent is done so clear the second floor then get out so we can fight this thing with all we've got."

"Roger that," I say, locking eyes with my brother. He moves closer, his expression telling me he's not pleased, but we have to follow orders —especially from the Captain. We've got no choice. Pierce may be the biggest asshole I know, but he's still a firefighter. He's bound by the same principles and oath we all are. When we're putting our lives on the line, we have to be able to trust each other.

A moment later, Pierce appears at my side, a nod between us serving as our silent and muted greeting.

I follow him up the stairs, stopping by his side when we reach the top.

"Split up and we can clear it quickly between the two of us. If anyone was here, we'd know about it by now anyway. The vent is done. As long as we don't cause a backdraft, we'll be fine. Okay?" he yells, leaning in close as the house creaks and groans.

"Together, Pierce. Never leave another man alone, *remember?*" I say.

He nods and I can tell it's a conciliatory gesture, but I take it as an affirmative nonetheless. I don't miss him grinding his jaw though.

Pierce sweeps his arm ahead. "Behind you, Lieutenant."

We clear the first room together, finding no one. I focus on the job at hand, keeping my wits about me in the face of danger.

Pushing on, we move to the next room near the front of the house, but as soon as I step inside, something is wrong. There's a change in the air, and Pierce is nowhere to be seen.

That's a second before my entire world implodes as the window in front of me shatters. Something is thrown from behind me.

I'm stuck relying on my training to save myself. The door behind me slams shut but it's too late. It blasts back open, and all I can do is drop to the ground and hope for the best. Halfway down, I'm thrown against the wall with a deafening thud before falling down face-first, the lip of my helmet hitting catching before it's knocked free. My mask digs into my skin as I hit the deck, my forehead colliding with the floor.

Then everything goes black.

———

An alarm blares in the distance. It's muted, almost dull, but it's continuous and doesn't stop. My head wants me to ignore it, throbbing pain taking up most of my brainpower. My PASS device keeps sounding, droning on and on, just like the shouting voices coming from the radio which is wedged between the floor and my chest. *Probably why it hurts like a bitch too.*

I open my eyes, trying to get my bearings and work out what the hell happened and where I am.

My ears are ringing and my head kills. My SCBA feels like a dead weight on my back, and my mask is suffocating me. My helmet is gone, obviously knocked away when I fell.

There's a constant drone coming from my PASS device since I'm not moving, the long drone getting louder then softer, over and over again. "Marco? Motherfucking answer me, Lieutenant?"

I hear shouting coming from the radio but my head is still fuzzy and it's muffled beneath my chest. It takes everything I've got to shrug off the straps on one shoulder. I grunt and use all the energy I have to roll onto my side so I can reach the belt at my waist and jerk that off too, then it's back to my front, one more shoulder strap off, and my tank is gone, my mask soon following.

The yelling continues, but now that I can lie flat on my back, I can focus a little better. Losing the mask was against SOP, but without air in the tank, the mask was useless anyway.

I focus on the radio, recognizing the voice. It's familiar, like mine. Maybe my brother?

"Lieutenant Rossi, *copy?*" I'd recognize that voice anywhere. Rhodes.

"Rhodes." *Cough.* "Rossi copy?"

"Marco? Thank fuck," he replies. "You alright?"

"Head hurts. Air gone too. Was that . . ." *Cough.* ". . . a backdraft? Came right at me before I could do anything. Need . . ." I cough, my chest getting tighter and tighter. *Fuck, it's hard to breathe.* The air is so thick. Smoke fills the room, making it too dark to see much of anything. "Need . . . help," I croak.

"Where are you?"

"Second floor. End room."

"Yeah. Pierce called it in just before it happened. Is he with you?"

"Not . . . here," I say between hacking my lungs out.

"Stairs are out. Stay put, Lieutenant. Cap?" Rhodes says into the radio.

"Copy. What do you need, Rhodes?" our Captain replies.

"Ladder to the window. Send Scotty and Luc up quickly. The vent wasn't done right the first time."

"On it," Luca replies, not waiting for the Captain to confirm the orders. "Coming for you, brother. Stay put and don't do anything stupid. Mama will kill us otherwise."

I chuckle but it just makes me cough again.

"I'll just . . . stay here . . . and . . . wait," I grind out, trying not to breathe in like my body desperately wants me to do.

"Where's Pierce?" Rhodes asks. "Is he out?"

I frown as it all comes back to me. "He's . . . the one . . . who shut the door on me . . ." I rasp. "He . . . screwed me . . . didn't he?" *God. I forgot how much breathing smoke fucking sucks.*

"Motherfucker. I'm gonna kill the son of a—" Rhodes shouts down the radio before being cut off—probably by the Captain. He's not a stickler for proper radio use all the time, but if there's likely disciplinary action on the horizon, he'll do what he has to do to make sure our asses are covered.

"Lieutenant, it's Cap. Standard protocol. Sit tight. Cover your mouth if possible. If not, face down on the ground. Can you move?"

"Yeah, I can . . . a bit . . ." I try to survey my injuries. Working my way through my body, I brace myself up on my elbows and try to lift up into a sitting position, succeeding on the second try.

I pat around the ground. My fingers finding purchase on my discarded mask. I summon everything I've got left in me to push myself up so I'm slumped back against a wall. I think it's near the window, 'cause there's a thin sliver of light coming through the dark, smoky haze. I try to use my legs to stand, maybe get air from the window, but my body won't cooperate. There's just nothing left in me and my head is so fucking foggy, I'm struggling to think straight.

"Where are you?" Cap asks.

"By the window, I think. I'm not . . . sure," I croak.

"Sit tight, Rossi. Ladder's up and we're almost there," he replies.

I wrack my brain trying to work out what the hell happened. "Where's . . . Pierce?"

"He's just been pulled out by his crew. He got thrown when the stairs went but he's walking."

"He's okay then?"

"He's masked up. Looks like a gash on his cheek but nothing bad."

"Call it in, Cap." Anger and pain course through me in equal measure.

"You saying something happened?" he growls.

"Standard ops not followed . . ." I wheeze. Talking is making it worse, but the more clarity I get as my foggy brain clears, the more obvious the situation is. "Expected him to have my back. Should've known."

"They vented just as the window blew out at your side of the house."

"He screwed me. Something broke the window, then the door was closed but it blew back open . . ."

"Definitely a backdraft," Cap says. His tone is so low and menacing it scares me. That says a lot, considering I'm stuck in a room filled with smoke and can't even pull myself up to my feet.

My throat burns. Every time I swallow it feels like acid is being poured down it. "He wouldn't . . . listen to fucking reason and wait for the all-clear to go," I wheeze, the weight on my chest so fucking heavy, talking is impossible.

Then suddenly, the sliver of light turns into a billowing curtain of fresh air as my brother pushes through the window. His head turns my way. I reach up and grunt. His hand grabs my forearm, his eyes locking with mine.

"Got you, brother. Now if Scotty can find his balls and pull us back, we can get you out of here."

"Hey, I heard that, Luc," Scotty yells from outside.

Luca smirks at me. "Meant you to."

I use the last of my energy to roll my eyes. "Can we give him shit . . . *after* he's helped saved me?"

Luca grins. "*Fine.*"

"Then Mama won't have to kick your ass," Rhodes says down the radio.

"Cut the crap and get the hell out of there you two," Cap bellows, silencing the chatter.

I chuckle and start hacking my lungs out again, making Luca's grin turn into a frown. "Yeah, Cap . . ."

"See you down here, Lieutenant," Cap replies, signing off.

"Yeah . . . he'll get right on that, Cap. When he stops trying to win an Oscar," Luca says, leaning down and hooking his arms under my shoulders. Then I'm being jerked up, Luca taking my weight.

"Fuck. . .you" I whisper roughly.

"You act like you're dying or something," Luca says. "Since I know Mama *and* Renee would ride my ass if that happened, quit trying to get me in trouble like you always fucking do."

I force out a laugh but it just makes me cough again. "Sure thing, little brother."

"Good. Let's go." Then he's all business and within moments, I'm out of the window and sucking in mouthfuls of glorious fresh air like my life depends on it.

And there's only one thing—one person—on my mind. *Renee.*

Minutes later, Skye and Co hover over me. Skye's eyes are wet and she's muttering under her breath about stupid brothers and stupid fires. Cohen is all focus, taking my vitals and hooking up monitors before shoving an oxygen mask over my face.

"Luc?" I say, lifting myself on an elbow and jerking the mask away, locking eyes with my brother. Luca throws his hand out to stop Cohen shutting the bus's back door.

"Yeah?"

"Call Renee," I whisper.

He lifts his chin. "Already on it. Gio's gone to pick her up. We'll meet you at the hospital."

My eyes drift from Luca to a frowning Rhodes and a concerned Zach, finishing with an angry Captain whose responding nod gives me more reassurance than anyone else.

My body slumps back onto the gurney, any leftover tension leaches out of my body.

I wave my hand in the air half-heartedly and turn my head, giving my baby sister a gentle grin as she jerks the mask back over my face. Skye's narrowed eyes would make me laugh if it was any other time.

She points a finger at me. "Behave, Lieutenant. Otherwise, I'll sic Mama on you."

I close my eyes, the events of the last thirty minutes and what might've been finally weighing on me. "Not sure who's scarier—you, Mama, or Renee."

"My pick is your woman."

I snort but groan when pain shoots through my chest. "I think that's a pretty safe bet."

RENEE

My heart is racing, my mind going a million miles an hour as Gio leads me out of the elevator with a gentle hand at the small of my back.

When he knocked on my door an hour ago, I had to lock my knees to stop from falling over.

We walk through the doors and into the waiting area, the room full of Marco's crew and family. Mrs. Rossi jumps up out of her chair and envelopes me in a huge hug, and I lose the loose control I have on my emotions, burying my face in her shoulder and letting tears fall for the first time.

She rubs my back soothingly. "It's okay, Renee. He's just a bit banged up but he's going to make a full recovery. I promise you. You're strong enough to handle this. I know you are. My Marco wouldn't love a woman who wasn't."

I nod and she lets me go, leaving her hands on my shoulders and meeting my eyes, her gaze then roaming my face as if to make sure I heard her words.

"I think . . ." I say, sniffing and wiping my eyes, trying to pull myself together. "I think I'm just in shock. The last thing I expected was for him to get hurt. He's always so strong, so formidable."

Mama smiles at me, giving me a reassuring squeeze before letting me go. "My Marco is all of those things but he's still just a man, and I'll let you in on a secret," she says, leaning in and bringing her mouth to my ear. "All of the Rossi men are like that, but they also need a powerhouse of a woman at their back and sometimes their front. These things are sent to test us, but they're also the making of us."

I nod, biting my lip so I don't start crying again.

I square my shoulders and pull myself together, feeling the love and support of everyone in the room surrounding me, but also knowing they're here for Marco; their Lieutenant; their friend; their brother.

"Now, he's been asking for you, and I know he'll feel a lot better for seeing you," Mrs. Rossi says.

I huff out a big breath, desperately needing to see for myself that he's okay. "Don't you want to go in and see him first? I'm not family. I'm just his—"

One look at her determined face and I can see the mama bear within shining through. The woman who always had Marco's back before he met me is just as fierce and determined as the man himself. Then I remember what he told me about his mother being the one to teach the Rossi children how a woman should be treated, and his father being the one to show them. Respect. Honor. Love. The three corner-stones of my relationship with Marco. The three things he's shown me from the start.

I can do this. I can be the strong one until he's back on his feet and ready to take the reins again.

"Are you ready?" Gio asks, coming up beside me, Luca flanking my other side. Mrs. Rossi looks between her boys, reaching out to cup both their cheeks, pride shining in her gaze. She locks eyes with me, and I don't miss the significance of this moment. It's like she's handing the baton over, giving me the job of seeing to the man we both love.

I nod, silently promising her that I'm the only other woman for the job.

Gio and Luca walk with me down the corridor, leading me to Marco's room, nodding to a tall, very handsome doctor standing at the nurses' station outside, jotting notes down in a folder.

"Cade," Luca says, reaching out and shaking hands with him, Gio following suit. "This is Renee, Marco's partner."

"Hey," Cade says, holding out his arm to shake my hand. "He's a little banged up but he's going to make a full recovery. He's got a mild concussion and a little smoke inhalation from losing his mask. But he was pulled out as soon as they could get to him and will be able to go home tomorrow after some oxygen and monitoring overnight."

I don't know what comes over me, but I step forward and wrap my arms around the doctor's shoulders, hugging him tightly.

"Thank you, Doctor. I'll make sure he does everything he's told to do, even if I have to chain him to my bed to make him rest."

"Call me Cade, Rence. And he's lucky to have you. He's been asking for you ever since he was brought in. I hope he might finally be able to relax now that you're here."

"Don't you worry," I say, letting myself accept the fact he's going to be okay. "He knows not to argue with me. In fact, I know he hates it."

"You remind me of my wife. She's just as scary as you are," Cade says with a smile which says he doesn't mind one bit.

"You're a lucky man then."

"Believe me, that is something I do know." He shakes hands with Gio and Luca again. "I'll leave you guys to it. Just call out if you need anything."

"Will do, Doc. Thanks again," Luca says before turning to look down at me as Cade strolls down the hall.

"You ready?" Gio asks. "We'll leave you guys to it, okay?"

"You can come in. I'm sure he'll want to see you as well."

"Not as much as you, princess," Gio says, tapping my nose. "We'll see him after."

Luca nods in agreement. "Now go. Marco is not the best patient, and right now, he's downright grumpy."

"Okay, thank you. For coming to get me, and being here."

"Renee, you're family. The only one who doesn't seem to get that yet is you," Luca says, his eyes crinkling at the sides. "We'll be in the waiting room if you need us."

I don't wait any longer. I open the door to the room with M. Rossi on the side and step inside, closing it behind me and getting my first look at the battered but well and truly alive love of my life.

He smiles when his eyes meet mine.

"Come here, baby," he rasps, holding his hand out and I'm at his side before he's finished talking.

"You're in so much trouble, Lieutenant," I say, my voice breaking as I gently run my hands over his arms, shoulders, chest, and then up to his face.

"I'm okay. It got a bit hairy but I'm good now, especially 'cause you're here."

He lifts his arm and I don't even question him, carefully easing myself into the bed beside him, draping my body over his.

"Feeling a lot better now," he rumbles, before coughing and trying to clear his throat. I shift to get off him and he grips my hip to hold me in place. "You're not going anywhere. Need you close."

Pressing my cheek to the pillow beside his head, I meet his eyes, letting my hand rest over his heart to reassure myself he's okay.

"So, what happened? Gio wouldn't tell me much except you got trapped and they had to get the ladder up to pull you out."

"That's pretty much it. We got told the vent was done except it was called too early. Then something happened, got caught in a backdraft, lost my helmet and mask, and got a good knock to the back of the head. Came to, found my radio, called out for help, and Luca and Scotty hauled me out the window."

I lean in and move his mask aside for just long enough to brush my lips against his before putting it back on, loving the soft, lazy look he gives me.

Resting my forehead against his, I take a huge breath, embracing the growing lump in my throat. "I can't lose you, Marco. We just found each other; we've got a lifetime to make up for."

"Princess," he says, his voice thick. "I'm not going anywhere, and I'm not letting anyone or anything keep me from you." He wraps his arms around me and hugs me tight as I do the same.

"Good to hear." I sniff, as we sit there in peaceful silence, soaking each other in.

Then all hell breaks loose outside, Luca's angry growl breaking the tranquility.

"You have some fucking nerve, Pierce. You don't deserve to wear that uniform."

I push myself up on an arm in the bed, my eyes going to the door before swinging back to Marco, who eyes me warily. That sets off alarm bells in my head and I quickly think over his explanation, my mind catching on things he didn't say.

My blood boils, my muscles tensing. Marco's eyes widen. "Baby, no. Do not—"

Grams warned Marco I was hell on wheels when angry, and something tells me I'm about to hit the stratosphere. "Please tell me that Nick Pierce had nothing to do with this." My voice is low and rough, my anger reaching a fever pitch when Marco clamps his mouth shut and rubs his hand up and down my arm as if to try soothe me.

"No," I say, my eyes stinging with tears but for an entirely different reason because there's a haze clouding my vision now and its color is red.

I scramble off the bed. Marco reaches out to stop me but I'm too fast and too determined to catch.

Marco jerks off his oxygen mask. "Princess, no. He's not wor—"

With my hand on the door handle, I whirl around to look back at him over my shoulder. "He's a worthless son of a bitch who almost got you killed. And for what? Because of a bruised ego? Because you punched him when he was an asshole to me? Because he thinks you're playing with his toys?" I screech. "No. I almost lost you, Marco. He doesn't get to do that, and he needs to know that."

"He'll get what's coming to him," he says roughly, his throat still raw.

"Yes. He will," I say, my tone menacing and deceptively calm. I point to the bed. "You, stay."

Marco quirks a brow, his lips twitching. "Really?"

"Yes," I demand. I cross the room and bend down, touching my lips to his. "You defended me. Now it's my turn to repay the favor."

"You don't have to."

I lift my head and shoot him a 'Really?' look.

When he slumps back down into the mattress I know I've won this fight. "Just don't do anything I would do."

"Believe me, I'm going to do *exactly* what you'd do."

He gives a resigned sigh. "I figured."

"Don't worry, Lieutenant. I'll leave the door open so you can watch."

"Just don't make my brother arrest you," he says. I swear I catch the smallest of smiles when I blow him a kiss.

Then I let my anger fly free and stalk out of the room, finding Rhodes, Luca, and Zach in the middle of the corridor, facing off against Nick. Gio is leaning back against the nurses' station, staring daggers while Rhodes and Zach struggle to hold back an angry Luca. Further down the hall is Marco's Captain, standing with his arms crossed, glaring at the confrontation but not making a move to control his men. That in itself speaks volumes and makes me more determined to tear my own piece of flesh from my ex-fiancé.

Gio's gaze swings to me, watching closely as I close the distance and storm around Luca, Rhodes, and Zach to get in Nick's face.

His eyes widen when he catches sight of me. "Nay, I just wanted to apologize."

"Oh, no. You don't get to call me anything anymore. As far as I'm concerned, you lost the right to talk to me five years ago when I called off the wedding, and you ceased to even exist the day I met Marco Rossi and knew what a real man was. And you," I spit out, poking my finger in his chest, "do not get anywhere near him or me or his family, because they're my family now and I'll defend them until my last breath. Even on his worst day, Marco is so much more of a man than you'll ever be."

Nick's eyes are narrowed slits, and I can feel the anger and hatred rolling off him, which proves what I guessed already—Nick Pierce is here to see his handiwork but also lay the foundation for what will likely be a long, drawn-out investigation, one in which he'll try to throw the man I love under the bus to save his own ass.

I cross my arms, my face screwed up as I shake my head. *What the hell did I ever see in him?* "You're a joke. You saw me with Marco and you couldn't stand it, so you tried to ruin my night at the ball, and when that didn't work and Marco embarrassed you, you decided to lose your ever-loving mind and try to kill him!"

"He's fine, isn't he?" he says. I glare at him, not believing what I'm hearing. There's no remorse at all. Nick is looking out for Nick and Nick only. Then he looks me up and down and sneers. "You two deserve each other. You're both as worthless as—"

I slap the last word out of his damn mouth before I'm jerked backward. Rhodes hooks his arm around my belly, holding me away from my shell-shocked ex, who's pressing a hand to his face and scowling at me.

"I want to lay charges," he says, glaring at Gio.

"And what's your complaint, Lieutenant Pierce?"

"She assaulted me," Nick splutters.

Gio looks around the group. "I must've missed it. Luca, did you see what happened?"

Luca crosses his arms over his chest, suddenly seeming clueless. "I didn't see a thing. How about you, Rhodes?"

"Nope. Not me."

"Oh for fuck's sake. You're all in on it." He glares at Gio. "I'll have your badge too. There'll be security footage."

"Give it up, Pierce," Marco says. My head snaps toward his hospital room door to find him leaning against the frame, as if watching the show. "You're fighting a losing battle you're never going to win. Resign. Save yourself and the department the embarrassment and time of having to investigate your criminal behavior and just leave," Marco says, his voice rough and quiet, but no less commanding.

Nick snorts and shakes his head. "It was an accident, Rossi. I'm not going to sacrifice my career."

Marco rolls his eyes, looking to me before turning his attention back to Pierce. "Fine. Draw it out. Won't do you any good. There are witnesses. There's a record of past behavior and complaints made against you. I guarantee any investigation will end with termination at best and the filing of attempted murder charges at worst. So the ball is in your court. Just know this is done. I'll never work a scene with you again and I know the department will never stand for that."

Nick still won't give up. He drags his angry eyes from Marco back to me. "You two deserve each other," he snarls.

"Lieutenant Pierce," Marco's Captain announces, stepping into the fray. "You need to leave. But some advice—get in touch with your union rep because an investigation has been launched, and I have every faith that you'll be found guilty and terminated."

"All because of this bitch," Nick spits out, shooting daggers my way. I smirk and walk over to Marco, wrap my arm around his waist and stand by his side. "Yeah, Nick. It was about Marco but you made this about me. And news flash: I'm his bitch now, and he'll always be more of a firefighter and more of a man than you could ever wish to be. So give up, and if you're smart, you'll fall on your sword and resign."

"Fuck this shit," he says before turning around and stalking back down the corridor, all of us standing there and watching until he disappears from sight.

"Renee," Marco says, his raspy voice laced with humor.

I tilt my head to meet his eyes. "What?"

"A slap? Really?"

I wave my hand in the air, wriggling my fingers. "I wasn't going to risk hurting myself—not for him. He's not worth it," I say. "Besides, I figured a bitch like that deserves a bitch slap from the woman he always underestimated."

"Fuck," he says, dragging his hand up into my hair and crushing his mouth to mine. He chuckles against my lips. "You're one of a kind, princess—you know that?"

I smile and melt into him. "As long as you know that, then that's all that matters."

"Known it since the moment I met you."

I pull back and quirk a brow. "So you're buying a ticket?" I say, remembering back to that night at my front door when he laid all his cards on the table.

"I knew you were the one that first time when you knocked me on my ass," he says, shooting me a cocky grin. "And you reminded me why when you stormed out to slap some sense into Pierce."

"I was defending your honor."

"And I love you even more for that fact."

"Well, good," I huff.

"Baby?"

"Yeah?"

"We're moving in together. You know that, right?"

I tilt my head and quirk a brow. "Is that a question or a demand?"

"It's a forgone conclusion," he says, matter-of-factly.

"Then yes, I do know. I'd already decided the same thing when I saw you in that hospital bed."

"Good, because I *really* like your bed."

I arch a brow. "And me in it with you too, right?"

"Yeah, baby. That too." Then I can't say anything else because he's kissing me again, and I'm definitely not going to argue about *that*.

EPILOGUE

Marco

It's been two months since I got caught up in that house fire and one month since the investigation concluded. As Cap had warned him, Lieutenant Nick Pierce was fired. I declined to press criminal charges against him and the last anyone heard was that he'd left Chicago, destination unknown. The general consensus was that he wouldn't be missed. One thing is for sure—I definitely felt better attending a call-out with Engine 22 and knowing I could trust Alex, their new lieutenant, to have my back and my guys' backs if needed.

The other thing that happened since then has been a bit of living situation switcheroo. Given the option of staying or going, Gio opted to stay and live in my house by himself. He said he might end up getting a roommate at some stage, but in the meantime, he's happy to have his own space without—in his words—"walking into the living room and cock-blocking my brother."

The other change was Hayley moving out of Renee's duplex and in with Grams. To her credit, Grams tried to protest and say that she didn't need a babysitter, but she admitted to Renee that she felt a little better knowing that Hayley would be there just in case anything happened. Although, they did both agree to not encroach on each other's social lives, which included Hayley not bringing men home, and Grams promising not to cause any trouble when her 'girls' came to visit from out of state.

And today, after months and months of training, Firehouse 101 is facing Firehouse 22 and other teams in the Tough Mudder, with the winning crew earning bragging rights, and all money raised going to the winner's chosen charity. In this case, we've agreed that if either house wins, Big Brothers Big Sisters will receive the donation regardless.

"You ready for this?" Renee asks as we walk hand in hand toward the start area.

"Hell, yeah. We're determined to come out on top, and we've got a secret weapon up our sleeves that we didn't have last year."

"Oh, really? And who's that? Don't say Scotty, because I won't believe you," she says with a laugh.

I shake my head. "Don't count him out. He's stubborn and for all his faults, he never leaves a man behind. Which is good for a team event like this, he'll make sure we all get through an obstacle before moving on."

"Maybe I misjudged the guy," she says, as we make a beeline to where our crew are all standing around in a circle.

I give her hand a squeeze. "Scotty Jones is a lot of things, but he's one of the most loyal and dependable men I know."

"Maybe Hayley should've given him a chance after all."

"Oh, no. Your sister would spit him out and eat him for breakfast. The best thing she could've done was blow him off after their one-night stand."

"Um . . . it might've been *two* one-night stands."

I turn and stare at her. "No wonder he thought he was in with a chance. She led him on a bit."

She winces guiltily. "Yeah. Hayls has a habit of moving past anything and anyone that could be good for her, mainly because she has this image in her head of the perfect man and she's vowed to never give up until she finds him."

"And until then?"

"She's happy living life on the single-and-always-ready-to-mingle train."

I chuckle, Renee joining in when her words sink in. She gives me a gentle elbow bump. "I didn't mean it like *that*."

"Princess, any time you want to get *off* on my train, just say the word and hop onboard."

"Oh my *god*. That was terrible."

I grab hold of her head and touch my lips to her temple. "And yet I guarantee you're thinking about jumping me, aren't ya?"

"You're incorrigible."

"And yet, I'm the lucky S.O.B. who gets you all to myself."

She beams up at me. "Yep. But only if you win today. If you lose to 22, then I'm thinking you'll be *far* too tired for *any* post-race celebrations tonight."

"Just you watch, princess."

"I will. Speaking of that, I should let you go. I see our little Firehouse 101 cheerleading crew over there, ready and waiting."

I look over and spot my family, Grams, Hayley, Skye, Cohen's brothers and their families, and Ezra and Gilly. "I'll walk you over," I say, changing direction..

After greeting everyone and giving Mama, Grams, Hayley, and Skye a kiss and a hug, I move to Ezra and Gilly, shaking Ezra's hand. "This is a surprise. I didn't expect to see you two here."

"We met with Renee earlier in the week to sign the sale documents for the apartment and Wicker Park place, and she mentioned you and Cohen were doing this today, so we figured we'd come along too."

"Awesome. Thanks. I'm surprised Renee didn't hit you up for a donation too," I say, stepping away from the main group.

Ezra laughs. "Don't worry, she did. But it's all for a good cause, and better yet, tax-deductible."

Gilly rolls her eyes. "Ignore my husband. He'd donate regardless."

"Ez here probably wants to see me fall on my ass and get a mouthful of mud."

"That's just an added bonus," he replies with a smirk.

"I was actually meaning to catch up with you for a beer soon," I say.

He quirks a brow. "You need some plans drawn up?"

"Not at all—it's more to ask a favor. Your sister, Delilah. How is she doing?"

"Good . . ." he answers slowly, obviously wondering why I'm asking. I stand beside him and hook an arm over his shoulders, pointing over toward my crew and where Rhodes and Jake are standing.

"See the tall guy over there with the teenager standing next to him?"

"Yeah?"

I turn back to look him in the eye, Gilly's lips slowly curve up, and if ever I doubted the existence of women's intuition, I don't now. "That's Rhodes, my best friend, and his son, Jake. He lost his wife five years ago and it's just been him and Jake since then, and it seems that he's finally open to the idea of dating again and has been sneakily watching episodes of a certain YouTube cooking channel."

"Okay. So he watches Dee's videos. Is he a bit of a fan?" Gilly says, almost sounding giddy. "Because I'm sure we can arrange a meeting or something. We've got Skye and Cohen's BBQ coming up in a few weeks. I can just invite her along. If she's not working or filming, she's spending time with my nephew, Harvey."

"That sounds like a good start," I say, earning a confused frown from Ezra but Gilly is all smiles, her eyes twinkling with mischief and understanding.

She winks at me. "I see what you're doing, Marco, and I approve. It seems like matchmaking runs in the Rossi family."

I hold my hands up. "I don't know *what* you're talking about, Mrs. Baker. But if you want to help me the same way you helped Skye get Renee to give me a chance, I'm not going to say no."

"We'll talk. Okay?" she replies.

Ezra just laughs and shakes his head, wrapping an arm around his wife. "I don't wanna know. I'll let you two play cupid. All I care about is that he treats her right and makes her happy."

"He's one of the best men and fathers I know."

Ezra reaches out and shakes my hand. "That's what I needed to hear." He gestures behind me. "I think you better get over there. The race is about to start."

"Shit. Okay. We'll catch up afterward," I say, looking around and finding Renee talking to Grams. I quickly walk to her and lean down to give her a kiss.

"Good luck, Lieutenant," she says, bringing her mouth to my ear. "If you win, I'll let you do anything, anywhere, anytime."

I pull back and grin at her. "You're on, princess." Then I jog over to the crew to warm up and make sure we're all stretched and ready to go.

When we hear the five-minute warning, we move to the start line, shake hands with the members of Firehouse 22, and wait for the starter's gun.

For the record, it was neck and neck between 22 and 101 right up until the last obstacle—the Texas Hold'em—where team members have to pair up and shuffle along a see-sawing triangle platform that moves and shakes back and forth with even the smallest of jerks. It came down to the last pairing of Jake and myself, with Engine 22 edging ahead halfway through. But with our little cheerleading team yelling and cheering for us on the sidelines, and our crew egging us on and screaming at us to 'move our asses' and 'hurry the hell up,' Jake and I pushed and pulled, growled and grunted, and with our muscles burning and our legs aching, we rallied right till the end. Our hands gripped together and we lifted them high in the air as we collapsed across the finish line with a five-second margin over our just-as-tired rivals.

I'm barely back on my feet when I see a flash of movement coming at me, and I just have time to brace myself before Renee jumps up into my arms, not giving a single shit that I'm wet and covered in mud from head to toe. Then she grabs my face in her hands and slams her mouth down on mine for a hard, long, deep kiss for the ages.

"You ready to go home, Lieutenant?" she asks breathlessly when we finally pull apart.

"I am now that you've got a promise to follow through with."

"Aww, you sure you're not too tired?" she asks, her lips quirking into a deceptive smile.

I squeeze her ass and hold her to me as we walk our way over to the stage where the prize-giving is going to be held. "As soon as we get our trophy, I'm taking you home. I'll never be too tired to lay back and watch you do all the work, princess. It's time for you to sit on your throne."

THE END

Up next – Rhodes and Delilah's story in Life Changer where we'll see the single, divorced mom and our favorite widowed, single dad get another chance at getting their own happy ever after. Preorder HERE

CHICAGO FIRST RESPONDERS SERIES

Life Changer – Rhodes and Delilah

Miracle Worker – Gio Rossi

Rule Bender – Luca Rossi

———

Sign up for release alerts and Series information HERE

Want to read Skye and Cohen's story:

Keep reading for Chapter 1 of Game Saver

It's one of those cliché moments. Our eyes meet across the bar, a lightning spark buzzing between us and—speaking for myself—one that shoots straight through me. I watch him lean over to say something in his friend's ear then make his way through the crowd toward me.

The first thing he says isn't what you'd expect from a man like him; he's good looking, well dressed, and definitely not hurting for money or choices when it comes to women. He doesn't say "Hey" or "Can I buy you a drink?"—which all women know is code for "I'm trying to get in there." No, the first words he says to me are "Nice shoes . . ." as he methodically undresses me with his eyes, a slow-growing cocky grin making his already pretty face downright gorgeous.

It's a bold move, but a very effective one.

"What will it take to get the rest of the pickup line?" I ask, twirling the tip of my drinking straw with my tongue. His gaze drops to my lips, his eyes darkening before lifting to meet mine.

"A taxi ride to your place."

Just. Like. That. My heart pounds, my panties melt, and those six words send a thrill through me. He's a guy who knows what he wants and how to play the perfect game to get it from me.

"You don't think we should do the mature thing and get to know each other first? Maybe share our deepest, darkest secrets or something?" I tease.

With one elbow to the bar, the other resting on the back of my bar stool, he leans into me—total personal space invasion—and brings his lips to my ear. "Right now, I'm interested in what's underneath that fucking dress and how fast I can make you come the first time. The second will be a test of your stamina, and if you can still talk after number three, then we can talk about anything you want."

Goddamn. This man's like my dream guy, but dirtier and overly confident in a way that presses all my buttons.

Standing up straight, I find myself fascinated by his mouth, wondering what his lips would feel like if I kissed him. What will they taste like, and how will he use them to follow through on the wicked promises he just made?

I want it. I want him. I'm not a girl with hang-ups but I don't just go home with random guys willy-nilly. I'm a "take it or leave it" girl. If I'm in the mood and have a connection with a guy, I'll go home with him but always to their place. That way I can slam, bam, and 'get my ass out of there' ma'am. Then, unless I want to see them again, they have no idea how to find me.

Safety first, condoms, and no strings unless you tie them yourself—they're the three things my hippie mom has drilled into me. "Free love makes the world go 'round, Abi-Jane, and everyone needs to feel loved at least once in their lives."

Right now, I've decided to roll the dice and take a chance on this good looking, well dressed, obviously well off guy who's making dirty promises I can only hope he'll keep.

I finish the last of my cocktail and turn around to find him towering over me. Tall, maybe six foot two, wearing a fitted black button-down that clings to his chest and arms in such a way that you know it's tailored just for him. His eyes are gentle, sapphire blue, his hair a dirty brown with a flash of auburn. He's gorgeous and is mine for the taking. So, I decide to indulge.

"Your place or mine?" I ask, shocking myself at the invitation.

"Yours," he says gruffly, taking a step forward and wedging himself between my thighs, my dress riding up as he moves in.

"I know this is a sex club, but remember the saying 'lady in public, whore in the bedroom' . . . ?" I ask with a quirked brow.

"And what would you do if I slid my hand under your dress and slowly inched my fingers between your legs . . ." I'm startled at the touch of his warm skin against mine, exactly where he described. I'm panting now and my heart is trying its best to beat its way out of my chest.

His voice drops low, for my ears only as he continues, "Will you fight your body's instinct to squirm and moan while you gently ride my fingers . . . right . . . here . . ." His hand dips under my dress, his thumb taunting me over my panties.

I reach up and grab hold of his shoulders, snagging his cropped hair in my fingers and pulling him down to me. "If you're trying to test me, you're going to have to do a lot better than that."

"I always win a challenge, little spitfire," he says, unfortunately moving his hand back to a more appropriate place.

Deciding this party for two needs to move on to a more private location, I slide off the stool, brushing my body against his, and get a thrill when he doesn't step back.

I stand next to him, his eyes scanning me top to bottom and back again, as I show him that I'm not, in fact, little, my heels taking me to almost his height. "Big spitfire . . ." he muses, his lips curving up on one side and revealing a dimple that begs to be licked.

"Are you always so forward?" I ask, resting a hand on his hip lightly without thought. It's not a calculated move. It feels natural. Needed . . .

"Are you always so receptive to the advances of men who don't fuck around when they see something they want?"

"Only good looking, well dressed ones who act on it."

"That works for you?"

"So far, it's you that's working for me. Whether that pans out or not is up to you . . ." I throw down the gauntlet, and my body itches to see whether he'll rise to the challenge—and all the creative ways he can do it.

"Say goodbye to your friend . . . ?" He jerks his head toward my best friend Amy—the reason why I'm here alone—and inadvertently gives away just how closely he's been watching me. Raising his brow, he waits for me to comply.

"Abi," I say, taking my hand back and offering it out to him.

"Cade," he rumbles, his voice deep and rough, a sound that could drive you higher or bring you back down. It's one of those tones you could fall asleep to, climax from, and listen to forever.

What he does next rocks me to the core. He doesn't shake my hand; instead, he gently wraps his fingers around mine, lifts them up to his mouth, and places a whisper-soft kiss on each of my knuckles, elevating my orgasm detonation level skyward with each new touch. A shiver courses through me from the tips of my toes, up my legs, through my chest, then down to my fingertips. That sexy, slow-growing smile of his widens when my hand trembles in reply.

Remembering the adage of safety first, I turn to the bar and whistle to grab Amy's attention. She finishes pouring a line of shots then comes my way, leaning in close, her eyes doing a sneaky scan of the man holding my hand and standing at my side before returning to me.

"Are you leaving?" she asks. Captain Obvious.

"Yeah."

"Everything good?" she presses, her eyes flicking toward Cade.

"They will be in about twenty minutes' time if the promise of him is—in fact—a sign of very good things to come my way."

"You going to his?" she says quietly.

"Mine."

Her eyes bug out and she gasps. "Babe . . . you sure?"

"Yep. Look at him. My creep radar has not pinged once. He's hot, he's forward—but no more than me—and his confidence is intriguing as fuck. I'll text you tomorrow." She moves her head back and studies me.

"Are you drunk?" she continues.

I grin. "Nope."

"Is Dani home?"

"Yep."

Cade says nothing through all of this; he just stands beside me, the heat radiating off his body warming me like a slow-burning fire that could roar to life at any moment.

"You better text me," she warns, just as Cade squeezes my hand. "Got to go." She turns her head for me to kiss her cheek like I always do, although I don't miss her sneaky head-to-toe scan of Cade at the same time. When I stand up straight again, I look at the fine male morsel before me and grin wickedly. This is gonna be fun. "Shall we go?"

"You lead, I'll follow."

"From what I've seen so far, I'm guessing that's the only time that's gonna happen tonight?"

"You're a quick learner, Spitfire. Let's go so I can see you ignite with a bang."

"Promises, promises," I whisper as I lead Cade away from the bar, his hand resting on my back, his fingers just dipping inside my low-cut dress.

Thankfully we score a cab right outside the door. Even better is Cade's mouth hitting mine for the very first time the second the car pulls away from the curb.

For the record, I was right. There was no leading required. Cade takes control and plays my body the way he wants. Four times. In one night. Then again in the morning.

That was the only time we hooked up . . . until last night.

Last night, everything changed. Whether that's a good thing or not is yet to be seen.

All I know is I've reviewed the forecast, and I'm predicting orgasms.

ABOUT THE AUTHOR

BJ Harvey is the USA Today Bestselling Author of the Bliss Series. She also regards herself as a smut peddler, suspense conjurer and a funny romance thinker upper. An avid music fan, you will always find her singing some hit song badly but loving every minute of it. She's a wife, a mom to two beautiful girls, and hails from the best country in the world—New Zealand—but currently lives in Perth, Australia.

Join my FB readers group "Harvey's Harem"

Facebook

Instagram

Goodreads

Sign up for her mailing list here

ALSO BY BJ HARVEY

The Bliss Series

Temporary Bliss (Bliss #1)—Mac and Daniel

True Bliss (Bliss #2)—Kate and Zander

Blissful Surrender (Bliss #3)—Sean and Sam

Permanent Bliss (Bliss #4)—Wedding Novella

Finding Bliss (Bliss #5)—Noah and Zoe

The Game Series

Game Player (Game #1)—Matt and Mia

Game Maker (Game #2)—Zack and Danika

Game Saver (Game #3)—Cade and Abi

Game Ender (Game #4)—Thomas and Amy

Game Breaker (Game #5)—Cameron and Sarah

Game Planner (Game #6)—Jase and Natalie

Cook Brothers Series

Work in Progress—Jamie and April

Work Violation—Jax and Ronnie

Working Back—Bry and Faith

Hard Work—Cohen and Skye

Working For It—Ezra and Gilly

Romantic Suspense

Lost in Distraction (Lost #1)

Lost For You (Lost #2)

Lost Without You (Lost #3)

Crave

Contemporary Romance

One Shot (Chances #1)

Second Chance (Chances #2)

Third Strike (Chances #3)

Touch (Sovereign Part One)

Taste (Sovereign Part Two)

Feel (Sovereign Part Three)

Made in the USA
Columbia, SC
15 September 2020

20651174R00124